"Let's play doctor."

Sam turned his back to Megan. "You can treat me first. I think I must have pulled a muscle."

Seductively Megan rubbed her palm over his shoulder. "Isn't part of the game to get the patient to undress?"

"Aha, now we're getting somewhere." He stripped off his shirt willingly, only to discover that the feel of her small hands on his bare back was sheer torture. If she knew what her nearness was doing to him . . .

But Megan was having problems of her own. Touching him, feeling his supple body beneath her fingertips made her long for greater contact. Her hands began to shake with the intensity of her desire.

Feeling the tremors, Sam turned to face her. "Doc?" he murmured. "It's my turn now, and I have a cure for what's ailing both of us. . . ."

MARIS SOULE
is also the author
of this title in
Temptation

LOST AND FOUND

SOUNDS LIKE LOVE

MARIS SOULE

MILLS & BOON LIMITED
15–16 BROOK'S MEWS
LONDON W1A 1DR

First published in Great Britain in 1987 by
Mills & Boon Limited, 15–16 Brook's Mews, London W1A 1DR

© Maris Soule 1986

ISBN 0 263 75749 8

21-0587

Printed and bound in Great Britain by
Cox & Wyman Ltd, Reading

1

IT WAS a quiet Friday afternoon.

Too darn quiet, thought Megan McGuire, her gray eyes scanning the nearly empty bar. She shifted to a more comfortable position on the padded bar stool and looked back down at the ledger open on the counter. How she wished she could will the credits to exceed the debits. Running her fingers through her short, dark brown hair, she tried to figure out why they weren't attracting more customers. It was the Friday before the Fourth of July, and The Quarter Note should have been busier.

When the new bar had opened on the opposite side of the lake, Megan and her father had known The Quarter Note's business would be hurt. What they hadn't known was that that bar, with its loud synthesized music and scantily clad barmaids, would become the "in" place to be around Shady Lake. If their own business didn't pick up soon, they would be in real financial trouble.

The telephone rang, and her father answered it in his office before Megan could stir from her stool. Her concentration interrupted, she reached for her glass of Coke. Just then the front door opened.

A slash of bright light cut through the dimly lit barroom. Blinking against the glare, her hand poised in mid-air, Megan tried to make out more than a silhouette.

She saw a mass of unruly curls, but she had no doubt that a man, not a woman, was standing in the doorwa̶

Nothing about his features was feminine. His face was a study in planes and angles, and a clean shave revealed the strong lines of his jaw. Dark-rimmed sunglasses covered his eyes.

He was dressed in attire typical of anyone staying at the lake. A bright blue cotton sports shirt was tucked into tight-fitting jeans—faded denims that hugged narrow hips and seemed to go on forever. He wore tennis shoes, the blue wave on the sides matching the color of his shirt. Megan didn't think she'd ever seen him before, but then, during the summer, tourists came and went faster than she could keep track of them.

Megan guessed his age to be about thirty. As the door swung shut behind him, he removed his dark glasses and slowly looked around the dimly lit room. She was certain his eyes would be blue, though whether dark or light she couldn't tell from where she sat. She realized, then, that she was staring, but couldn't stop herself—he had such an interesting face. One she would love to draw.

There was an air of self-confidence to his steps as he strolled toward the bar. Remembering why she was there, Megan slid down from her stool and moved behind the counter. "Still hot outside?" she asked, smiling.

"Like a steam bath." He wiped his arm across his forehead before returning her smile. "How about a cold beer?"

"What would you like?" Close as he was now, she could see his eyes were almost iridescent blue—dark on the outside, turning sky blue around ebony pupils.

"What do you have on tap?"

She named two popular brands; he chose one. She turned to pull a glass from the cooler, and as the cold beer streamed from the tap into the glass, she asked, "You just here for the weekend or staying on through the Fourth?"

"I don't know. Cash Barrigan playing here tonight?"

Megan grimaced and shook her head, bringing him his beer and taking the ten-dollar bill he offered. "Cash took off. He hasn't played here for over a week."

The old guitar player had gone without a word, leaving them in the lurch. Not that Megan had been surprised by his indifference to their situation. Long ago she'd learned musicians thought only of themselves and their careers. Still, Cash Barrigan's abrupt departure had caught them unprepared.

"Darn." The man in front of her frowned, his brow furrowing. He took a long quaff of his beer, nearly emptying the glass, then gave a sigh of relief and smiled. The harsh lines of his face softened immediately. "Would you believe it? I've been trying to catch up with that old guy for a month. He doesn't leave an easy trail to follow."

"Is he a friend of yours?" It seemed unlikely. Cash was a hillbilly, his Southern accent strong, and he favored corn whiskey and country music. The man facing her spoke with a cultured voice . . . with an almost foreign accent.

"No, I've only heard stories about him and his guitar. Know where he went?"

"No." She placed his change on the counter. "And I don't care," she mumbled under her breath.

He heard. "Do I note a bit of sarcasm there?"

Megan looked him straight in the eyes. "Do you know how hard it is to find a good musician around here?

"Next to impossible," she answered, before he had a chance to respond. "Now, if we were closer to Grand Rapids...or even Kalamazoo, it wouldn't be a problem. But here in Shady Lake, Michigan . . ." Megan shook her head and made a sound of disgust. "We can't even afford to pay quality players enough to make the drive back and forth worthwhile."

He glanced over at the corner of the barroom where a placard next to a piano announced that Joe Panche would be playing at nine o'clock. "Looks like you found *someone*."

Megan wrinkled her nose. "I suppose we should count ourselves lucky, but Joe's playing really isn't all that great." Thinking about Joe, she smiled. "However, he is darned good-looking, which does attract the women."

The man in front of her noted her smile and the absence of a ring on her left hand. "And interests one female bartender?"

"Me?" Immediately Megan shook her head. "No. Musicians don't interest me."

"That so?" His eyebrows rose in question as he pushed his empty glass toward her. "I'll have another."

"Coming right up." Megan turned her back to him, pulled out a cold glass and poured his beer. She liked the way he looked at her with those fascinating blue eyes. He intrigued her. Realizing she must have sounded rather abrupt, she offered an explanation of sorts. "I'm afraid past experiences have soured me on musicians. Besides, Joe's just a kid. I don't think he's more than twenty-two."

"You don't look much older than that yourself." She found him studying her closely when she turned to bring him his beer, his eyes traveling appreciatively down from the top of her head to take in as much of her as he could see behind the bar—then back up again.

Though over the years she'd come to realize men found her attractive, Megan wasn't really sure why. In her opinion her eyes were too wide set for her heart-shaped face, her nose too small and her mouth too full. And her hair absolutely refused to hold a curl, so she always ended up having it styled in a shag that made her look more like a pixie than the mother of a ten-year-old boy.

As for what this man was seeing of her body, Megan knew little of her figure was visible. Her slightly flared maroon skirt came just above her knees, showing a modest amount of leg, and although her short-sleeved white blouse had the first three buttons left open, it was topped by a maroon vest. Only a hint of the curve of her full bustline showed to entice a man's imagination. "I'm twenty-eight," she stated honestly, setting the frosty, beer-filled stein in front of him.

"A very attractive twenty-eight." He lifted the glass in a salute, his eyes never leaving her face. As his lips touched the rim, little butterflies fluttered in the pit of her stomach, and she would have sworn she felt the touch of his mouth on hers. It was really quite incredible.

Disconcerted, Megan lowered her gaze and began to count out the amount he owed her from the change he'd left lying on the counter. Without thinking, she licked her lips, almost expecting to taste a hint of beer. Turning away, she deposited the money in the cash register.

He's flirting with me and I'm letting my imagination run amok, that's all, she told herself. Not that it bothered her. After a year of tending bar she'd grown accustomed to men flirting with her. It was good for the ego, and sometimes she enjoyed flirting back, but she'd learned not to take them seriously. If this blonde was like most, he would flatter her a bit, probably tell her one or two suggestive stories, then leave. Sometimes one asked her out, but she usually refused. She didn't have time to get involved with a man.

"Tell me, what's a nice girl like you doing in a place like this?"

"Oh, brother—now there's an original line if ever I heard one," Megan said with a laugh, coming back to wipe a drop of beer from the counter. "Actually, I own The Quarter Note. Along with my father."

"You own this place?" He looked around curiously.

Old guitars and banjos hung on knotty pine walls, heavy drapes blocked out the glare of the afternoon sun and old-fashioned electric lamps provided subdued lighting. The tables were round and wooden, surrounded by mates' and captain's chairs, and the front bar was made of pine and topped with a wood-grained Formica counter.

The only patrons were three old fishermen, drinking beers and swapping stories about the one that got away; two middle-aged women, sipping margaritas and munching nachos as they talked; and a young couple in the corner, who were more interested in staring into each other's eyes than in drinking *or* talking.

"It's not much, but it's ours." At the moment she wasn't sure if she should boast, or lament the fact.

"Somehow you don't fit the image I have of a bar owner." His gaze returned to Megan's face.

"Which is?"

"The lady barkeepers I've known have either been built like Amazons or were as tough as nails." Once again his blue eyes raked over her slender, very feminine, five-foot-four-inch frame. "You don't fit either category."

"Oh, I'm tough enough," she said with a chuckle. She'd learned to be. But really she didn't think of herself as a barkeeper, either. As far as she was concerned, this was just a temporary situation, a chance for her to repay her father for all he'd done for her. Once The Quarter Note was on its feet, she'd go back to being a free-lance illustrator. That was the field she loved, what she'd studied in college and had worked at until a year ago.

But when the school where her father had taught for eighteen years closed because of declining enrollment, leaving him in his fifties, depressed and without a job, she'd been the one to suggest they pool their money and buy a bar. It had been a dream of his for years, a dream he might have pursued if it hadn't been for her. So she'd felt it her obligation to push him into a new career, and now she felt it her obligation to see that he succeeded.

"And what do you do if one of your patrons starts flirting with you?"

"It depends on who he is and if I want to flirt back," Megan teased, looking him directly in the eyes.

"You're not concerned for your safety?" The lift of his eyebrows showed his surprise.

With you, no, she wanted to say. He was tall, and if he wanted to, he could easily overpower her physically, but she wasn't afraid of him. She'd learned to read her patrons' characters by their facial expressions and body language. He was no threat. She realized, though, that his question had a deeper meaning. "If one of the customers gets too unruly, I call for help." She nodded toward the closed office door. "Not many are willing to take on my father. And when he's not around, there's Pete, our other bartender."

"So the lady is well fortified." His gaze held hers, even as he lifted his glass to his lips. A slight smile curved his mouth just before he took a drink, and when he put down the stein he leaned forward slightly, narrowing the distance between them. "Do I have to ask your father's permission?"

"Permission for what?" she asked coyly, pretending she didn't have the slightest idea what he might be talking about.

"For a date with you?"

"Ah, a date." So he was going to skip the suggestive jokes and sexual innuendos. She was glad. She much pre-

ferred a straightforward approach, and actually the idea
of going out with him was appealing. He had *such* an interesting face. "But I don't even know your name," she returned with a grin.

"Sam Blake." Politely he offered her his right hand.

Megan put down the towel and touched her fingers to
his. She had meant the contact to be brief, but found her
hand immediately surrounded by a strong, warm grasp.
A heated, tingling sensation flowed up her arm and invaded her body. Their eyes locked, and her breath caught
in her throat. She marveled at how alive she suddenly felt.

"And your name is?" he asked, his voice keyed seductively low.

"Megan," she rasped, totally aware that she was over-
reacting to a mere handshake, but unable to stop the
quivering in her stomach. "Megan McGuire."

"Megan," he repeated softly, still holding her hand. "I
like that. It fits you." His thumb caressed the back of her
hand. "You know you have beautiful eyes?"

"Do I?" she asked inanely, wondering how anyone with
iridescent blue eyes could think gray eyes were beautiful.

"Have dinner with me tonight."

"I can't," she groaned. "I have to work until ten."

"Then we'll make it a late dinner." His smile was be-
guiling.

Oh, how she wished she could. It would be fun to forget her worries, to dress up and spend a few hours being
wined and dined. But ruefully she admitted that was impossible. With a sigh, she removed her hand from his. "I
can't. I have a ten-year-old son. I have to be home with him
after work."

"And a husband?"

She could see him pull back, and respected him for that.
"No, no husband. My son and I live with my father."

Immediately he smiled. "Then how about tomorrow night?"

"Same problem. Getting a baby-sitter on a Saturday night is nigh unto impossible around here."

Sam chuckled. "Sounds like it's your son I'll have to get permission from. Do you ever have time to yourself?"

With a smile, Megan shook her head. "Not much, but perhaps tomorrow we could—"

She didn't finish her sentence. At that moment her father opened the door of his office and came out swearing.

Herb McGuire was just under six feet, burly and gruff looking. His size alone had deterred his high school math students from starting any trouble in class, and it served him well as a bartender. One glare from his steely gray eyes was usually enough to convince a troublemaker that a retreat was in order.

As a child, Megan had idolized her father. As a teenager, she'd rebelled against his strict rules. And when she was fifteen and her mother had died, Megan found herself at odds with him about everything. It wasn't until she was seventeen and pregnant that she'd discovered her father was the best friend she had. Now she loved him dearly and would do anything for him.

"Damn," Herb McGuire cursed a second time, on his way over to the bar.

"What's wrong?" Concerned, Megan turned to her father.

"That crazy Panche kid went and got into a car accident. I told him he drove too fast. But would he listen?"

"Is he . . . ?"

"He's all right. But he broke his arm. Damn!" Herb McGuire hit his fist on the counter, jarring several glasses.

"Left in the lurch again." Megan sighed, feeling the same anger and frustration her father was experiencing.

"I've tried all the names I had. There's no one willing to fill in for him tonight. One piano player seemed interested in working here, but not until after the Fourth." He glanced over at the piano. "Looks like the customers are stuck with me again. Can you work a double shift?"

"Who will stay with Josh?"

"Mrs. Arnosky?"

"Tonight's her bingo night."

"Can't he stay by himself for a few hours? I'll put him to bed before I come back."

"You know I don't like to leave him alone." Megan was afraid she'd have to give in, but hated the idea. She was away from her son too much as it was.

Grumbling to himself, her father ran thick fingers through his thinning, gray-streaked hair.

"Could I be of assistance?"

Sam's question caught both of them by surprise. Two pairs of gray eyes immediately turned toward him.

"Dad, this is Sam Blake," she introduced, certain her rather staid father would sometime or another make a comment about Sam's wild hair.

Herb McGuire's gaze took in both the blond stranger seated on the bar stool and his daughter. Although she was trying to act casual, Megan knew there was an unusual brightness to her eyes and a slight flush on her cheeks that her father had not missed. Curiously, he was now studying the man in front of him, no doubt wondering what had transpired before his interruption.

"If you just need someone for tonight," Sam went on, "perhaps I could help. I play the guitar."

A musician. Megan gaped at Sam, suddenly seeing him in an entirely new light. And to think she was considering going out with him. She almost shuddered visibly.

Her father noted her shocked expression. Sympathetically he tried to ease the man's let-down. "I'm afraid I can't take the loud noise those electric guitars put out. However, there's a new place on the other side of the lake. They might be able to use you."

Then he spoke to Megan. "Think you might be able to convince Mrs. Arnosky to give up her bingo tonight? If I'm on the piano, we'll really need you behind the bar."

Sam cleared his throat. "I'm not looking for a job, and I don't own an electric guitar. My singing's only so-so, but I've been told I'm a pretty good guitar player."

Herb McGuire looked back at him and his words were abrupt. "You ever played in a bar before?"

"A few times."

Probably as often as he can, Megan thought. She didn't like the idea that she'd been so entranced by a musician, but under the circumstances it seemed fortuitous that he was there. "Dad, you know nothing keeps Mrs. Arnosky from her weekly bingo game. I think we'd better hire him."

Even if Sam weren't a great guitar player, Megan was sure he'd be a better musician than her father. Not that she would ever come out and tell her father that, but anyone who'd listened to Herb McGuire's piano playing knew his repertoire consisted of a half dozen old-time favorites that he played over and over. Even the regulars begged for something new by the end of the night.

"I suppose you're right." Her father looked Sam up and down. "You'll start at nine, play forty-five-minute sets and finish at two." Then, as though to make certain his daughter didn't get a chance to completely ignore the man, he added, "You sign him up, Megan. I'm getting out of this place before we have another crisis."

"But, Dad," she cried, watching her father start for the door, "can't you do that?"

He forced back a smile and shook his head. "Nope. Time for me to get home to my grandson."

Megan sighed in defeat. "Tell Josh if he wants to stay up tonight, he can. I'll see him at ten."

As Herb McGuire was leaving The Quarter Note, the three men seated around the table called for another pitcher of beer. Megan was glad. It gave her an excuse to get away from Sam. Quickly she brought the men their beer, then checked on the couple in the far corner. Their drinks had been barely touched. From that table she moved on to the two women, but when she asked if they wanted another round they shook their heads and stood up to leave. Finally, no longer able to avoid it, Megan picked up the empty glasses and returned to the back of the bar. Sam was still nursing his beer.

"What hours do you work?" he asked, running the tip of his right index finger slowly around the rim of his glass, his eyes following her movements behind the counter.

"Two to ten." Her response was curt, and she avoided looking at him.

"How about having lunch with me tomorrow?"

"I'm busy" was her icy reply. She checked the two empty margarita glasses for lipstick, then dunked them into the sink and let the brushes give them an extra good cleaning before rinsing them.

"Breakfast?" he probed, sensing the change in her mood.

Her hands still in the water, Megan looked up at him. "Look, you're wasting your time. It doesn't matter what time of day, I'm not going out with you."

"Why?"

"Because I don't want to."

"You wanted to before your father interrupted us," he reminded her.

"Well, I changed my mind." It disturbed her to remember how close she'd come to setting up a luncheon date with him.

"Because I play the guitar?"

"Because it's my prerogative." Quickly she lifted the glasses from the sink.

"Don't you think I deserve some sort of an explanation?" Sam argued.

"No." Wiping her hands dry, Megan began looking for something to write with. By the cash register she found a pencil and pad of paper. She was all business when she came back to stand in front of him. "I'll need your full name and social security number. You do belong to the musicians' union, don't you?"

He nodded and frowned. "It is because I'm a musician, isn't it?"

Lowering her eyes, she ignored his question. "What name do you want on your check?"

"You were willing to go out with me before you found out I played the guitar, but now that you know I'm a musician, you don't want anything to do with me. That's ridiculous. I just don't believe it."

"Well, if you're not going to tell me different, your check will be made out to Sam Blake." She briskly wrote the name.

"Good enough," he growled.

"Address?"

"U.S.A."

Her head snapped up and she stared at him.

He shrugged his shoulders, his blue eyes decidedly cool. "You know how it is. We musicians are on the road a lot."

"Yes, I do know how it is, but I'll have to have an address. The IRS is fussy about things like that."

Sam gave her a Long Island address—whether it was real or phony she didn't know and didn't care—then his social security number and the other information she needed for her records. He mentioned that he was collecting folk songs, and she gathered he'd been on the road since May, moving from town to town, tracking down old musicians who played and sang little-known pieces. But what he was doing in Shady Lake didn't matter, Megan told herself. She wasn't interested.

Still, even as she tried to keep her eyes on the paper and her mind on her writing, she found it difficult to ignore him. He had beautiful hair, so thick and curly that it begged to be touched. And his eyes. How she wished she could find paint the color of his eyes. He moved his hands, and her gaze traveled from the paper to his fingers. Long, graceful fingers.

She noticed the nails on Sam's right hand were carefully manicured. Trimmed to a sixteenth of an inch from his fingertips, they were perfectly smooth. She knew that guitarists who played finger-style, rather than using a pick, had to keep their nails that way. Many even polished their nails with a hardener to keep them from chipping and catching on the strings.

"Is that what you'll be playing tonight? Folk songs?" she asked, putting down her pencil.

"I imagine your customers would prefer them to anything else I might play," he replied and finished his beer.

"Want another?" She pointed to his empty glass.

"No, two's my limit." Sam stretched and smiled suggestively. "I don't suppose room and board goes with the job."

"Definitely not," Megan said coolly, her eyes narrowing.

"No, I didn't think so. Any suggestions, then, on a place to stay?"

"Around here?" She paused to think. "Well, there's the Shady Lake Motel, but I doubt if they'll have a vacancy this weekend. In fact, I don't think you're going to find much available. Most people who come to the lake rent or own cottages."

She wanted to tell him to just leave after he'd finished playing, to go to Grand Rapids, Kalamazoo or Lansing. She didn't want to see him after tonight. She didn't like the way she couldn't seem to keep her eyes off him.

Picking up his dark glasses and the rest of his change, Sam slid off his bar stool. "I'll find something. You'll be here at nine, won't you?"

"Yes . . ." She drew the word out suspiciously, wondering why he wanted to know.

"Good." He winked at her, his long, blond lashes veiling the blue of his right eye for just a moment. "I think it's time someone proved to you that not all musicians are cads."

"Don't waste your time, Mr. Blake," she snapped, but a shiver of anticipation ran down her spine.

"Somehow I doubt if any time with you would be wasted." He winked again and smiled. "See you later."

Pete Henshaw was just coming in to the bar as Sam left. He was fiftyish, nearly bald and had a paunch that showed his love of beer. Pete had been bartending for them ever since they'd opened The Quarter Note, and Megan loved him as an uncle. As he came toward her, he was shaking his head. "Did you see the hair on that dude? Looked like he stuck his finger into a light socket."

2

SAM ARRIVED EARLY, carrying a guitar case. He'd changed into a black silk shirt, left open at the neck, tailored black pants and black leather boots. Despite her resolve to ignore him, the effect of the all-black outfit was striking, and Megan felt a strange curling sensation in the pit of her stomach when he approached the bar.

The Quarter Note was half full, most of the people regulars who came every Friday night, no matter who was playing. Two cocktail waitresses, both attractive and in their early twenties, had come on duty earlier and were tending the tables, while Megan helped Pete behind the bar. Setting a pitcher of beer, two glasses and a platter of crackers, summer sausage and cheese on a tray, Megan covertly watched Sam ease himself onto the bar stool in front of her.

"Hi," he said softly.

"Hello," she returned coolly. Looking beyond him, she motioned for one of the waitresses.

"Aren't you glad to see me?"

Megan's gray eyes narrowed as they met with his. "If you mean am I glad you showed up to work, yes. You're early, however."

"I wanted a chance to prove what a nice guy I am, that all musicians aren't alike." He grinned, and it was obvious he was ready to resume their earlier conversation.

"Ha!" she scoffed. "You'd need more than—" Megan glanced at her watch "—forty-five minutes to prove that."

"Then maybe I'll stay around for a while."

His voice was soft and seductive, his gaze mesmerizing, and Megan felt her pulse take off. She definitely did not like the effect he had on her. Abruptly turning her back to him to fuss with the bottles behind the bar, she tried to laugh off his warning. "You'll be an old man before I change my mind."

"Well, well, well," crooned a young woman's voice, "if it isn't the black knight. You're new here, aren't you?"

Immediately Megan felt herself bristle. Facing the barmaid standing next to Sam, Megan let her tone of voice make it clear she wanted no flirting. "Nancy, this is Sam Blake. He'll be playing here tonight."

"Playing what?" asked Nancy, ignoring Megan's warning and edging closer to Sam. Seductively she batted her false eyelashes.

"The guitar." He smiled at the impudent blonde. The ample contour of her bustline was obvious, despite the confines of her white blouse and maroon vest.

"Oh, I love the guitar," Nancy purred. Subtly she shifted her weight so her hip rubbed against his thigh. "And men dressed all in black. Tell me, is this for real?" Reaching up, she wound a golden lock of his hair around one finger.

"It's for real." He couldn't help laughing at the barmaid. "Sort of a trademark, like my clothes."

The sound of his laughter was rich and warm. That he was enjoying Nancy's coquetry bothered Megan. How could he come in here and make a pass at her, then let another woman play with his hair? "Nancy!" Megan snapped.

Slowly Nancy withdrew her finger from Sam's curly locks.

"Your order is ready." Megan's eyes were a steely gray.

Reaching for the tray, Nancy grinned impishly. "I'm going, I'm going."

Sam chuckled when Nancy gave him a final wink, and Megan fumed. Taking two empty glasses from the counter, she plunged them into the suds in the sink. "I know you're only here for one night, but as long as you're employed by The Quarter Note, there will be no flirting with the cocktail waitresses."

"I wasn't flirting, she was," he said, nonchalantly reaching over the counter to pluck a green olive from a nearby tray, "and I don't start work until nine, remember."

"A technicality."

He reached for another olive, and she slapped the bar mop across his knuckles. "Stop stealing the olives."

"I haven't had any dinner. Think you could fix me a sandwich?"

Without a word she handed him a menu that listed the variety of snacks they offered. He ordered crackers and cheese and a cup of coffee. Megan knew he was watching her unwrap the crackers and slice the cheese, but she pretended to be too absorbed in her work to notice. When she placed the plate in front of him, she was ready to squelch any smart remark he might make, but all he said was "Thank you."

Nancy took every opportunity to stop by the bar, asking Sam where he was from, where he was going and how long he'd be staying. Megan told herself she wasn't interested, then found herself listening. Not that she learned much more than what he'd already told her earlier that day.

When Nancy once again sashayed away from the bar, Megan slapped Sam's chit down in front of him. "Do you turn all women on when they meet you?"

Looking at her, he grinned. "I don't know. Did I turn you on when we first met?"

"Of course not." But she realized her question had betrayed her, and the color rushed to her cheeks. Clearing her throat, she changed the subject. "We never did discuss how much you should be paid for tonight."

"Whatever you would have paid the piano player will be fine."

Megan scoffed. "How do I know you're worth that much? I haven't heard you play yet."

He nodded solemnly, but there was a bit of a smile tugging at the edges of his mouth. "All right, then—you listen to me play and decide what I'm worth. Is that fair?"

"You'll take whatever I offer?" She eyed him suspiciously. Either the money meant nothing to him or he was desperate enough to take anything. By the looks of his clothes and the fact that he wasn't asking for a permanent job, the former assumption seemed the logical choice.

"Just what are you offering?" His eyebrows rose in question, his smile was suggestive and his blue eyes sparkled with amusement.

"You know what I mean," she said with a sigh, kicking herself for such a bad choice of words.

He chuckled. "Whatever you offer will be fine. Have you decided when we're going out?"

His question took her by surprise. "I thought I made myself clear. I'm not going out with you."

"But you didn't give me a good reason why."

"You're a musician."

"And all musicians are cads, right?"

"Right," she responded, wishing he'd simply drop the subject.

"Wrong," he said softly.

His gaze was intense, and for a moment she could do nothing but stare into his eyes, her legs feeling like lead. For eleven years she'd held on to one simple credo: *Don't repeat past mistakes*. During that time she'd dated an artist, a banker, a truck driver and an engineer. Never a musician. And not once had she questioned her reasoning. It had seemed simple. If you're burned once, you stay away from the fire.

But Sam Blake, a man she barely knew, was telling her she was wrong. And crazy as it was, she felt tempted to believe him.

"Well, maybe not all of you are cads," she murmured, unaware that she was leaning toward him. "But you've got to admit, your life-style isn't very stable."

"Mine's quite stable." Reaching forward, he touched the side of her face with the backs of his fingers. "Trust me, Megan. I won't hurt you."

As he gently caressed her cheek, Megan wondered if possibly she could trust him. There was something about him that was reassuring. He possessed an aura of self-confidence, of inner tranquillity, and a sense of purpose. Transfixed, she stood looking at him, not saying a word.

"Break it up, you two," interrupted Nancy, coming up beside Sam before either of them realized she was nearby. "I've got an order for three more beers and a bowl of pretzels."

Embarrassed, Megan jerked back. Even as she reached for the beer steins, she couldn't believe she'd actually been standing there enjoying the touch of Sam's hand. Perhaps besides being a musician he was a hypnotist. She still felt as if she were in a trance. When Nancy left with the beers,

Megan tried to shake off the sensation. "I don't know what it is you're trying to prove, Mr. Blake, but you're wasting your time." She glanced at her watch. "And speaking of time, you should start playing."

Sam grinned, his features taking on a strange charm that fascinated her. He nodded toward the exit door, back by the rest rooms. "Where does that lead?"

"Outside. We have our dumpster there. Why?"

"I want you to meet me out there during my break."

"No." She couldn't believe him. One minute he was asking her to trust him, the next suggesting a rendezvous.

Again reaching across the bar, he lightly tapped his fingertip against the end of her nose. "You've got to develop a more positive attitude, Megan McGuire. See you out there in forty-five minutes."

"No you won't," she called after him, but he continued to stroll across the room to the small platform with the piano and stool. *The nerve of the man! Meet him outside, indeed!*

He set his case down and opened it, pulling out a well-kept guitar. It was a graceful-looking instrument, with a fine-grained pine top and a delicately designed rosette around the sound hole. Certainly nicer looking than those hanging on the walls, with their warped necks and scratched tops. And quite different from what rock guitarists used—those electric instruments with their solid, lacquered fronts.

Sitting down on the stool, Sam positioned himself comfortably, one boot heel hooked on a rung, the other foot flat on the platform. At last he began to lightly pluck the guitar strings, his tuning barely audible above the din in the bar.

Megan watched every move he made, both fascinated and disturbed by her reaction to him. It wasn't as if she were love starved. She dated, when she found time. Usually the men who attracted her were the handsome, muscular type. And, in truth, Sam fitted neither category, although she did find his looks intriguing.

Also, with those she dated she wisely set rational limits to their relationships. After all, she had responsibilities—her son, her father and the bar. Attraction had to be tempered with reason. Today reason seemed to have left her.

Sam glanced up from his guitar, caught Megan watching him and smiled. Then a loud roll of chords announced to all that he was ready, and Sam Blake began to play.

Megan couldn't believe the sounds she heard. She wasn't sure what she'd expected. Perhaps the loud, strident music of most guitarists she had known produced, or the twang of strings that had marked Cash Barrigan's style, but neither was the case. Instead, lyrical strains reached her ears, and she felt herself drawn to the music.

It was a simple melody, reminiscent of many folk songs she'd heard in the past, but Sam was drawing out sounds from the depths of the instrument that Megan had never guessed a guitar could produce—beautiful, crisp, clear tones.

It didn't take an expert to recognize that he was good. More than good. Slowly the room began to quiet as people stopped talking to listen. By the end of his first piece, one could have heard a pin drop in the room. A moment passed before the customers realized he had finished, then the silence was broken by an explosion of whistles and clapping. Sam nodded, waited for the applause to subside and began to play again.

As she listened, the hairs on the back of Megan's neck seemed to stand on end and goose bumps ran over her skin. She shivered and tried to ignore the erotic effect of his music, but that was impossible. Under Sam's skillful touch a rich, warm rhapsody filled the room. She was mesmerized, as was everyone else in the bar.

He played familiar folk songs and some she'd never heard before. Occasionally he sang along, actually talking the lyrics more than singing them. His voice, deep and sonorous, was pleasing to listen to, and between pieces he began chatting with the customers, telling them a bit about the origins of each song.

Over a period of time the noise level in the bar rose, but never to its former pitch. People were listening, drinking and talking in hushed voices. Both Megan and Pete were busy as Nancy and the other cocktail waitress moved about the room taking orders and delivering drinks. New customers, visitors to the lake, came in and instead of leaving after one drink, stayed.

Sam finished his first set with John Denver's "Follow Me," and, as he sang the words, his eyes were on her. Megan felt herself tense. That song brought back such painful memories.

Once she'd followed a musician, leaving her father and all her friends behind. Rod Parrish had been everything a teenage girl dreamed about—good-looking, talented and sexy. He'd come to Grand Rapids to play at a rock concert, they'd met at a party, and *she* had fallen in love.

Megan shook her head, remembering that fateful night. "Follow me," Rod had coaxed. And he'd promised to take her to places she'd only dreamed about. Promised she'd never again feel alone.

And oh, how lonely she'd been since her mother's death. How confused and resentful. She'd felt her mother had deserted her. And her father, still trying to cope with his own grief, didn't understand.

One year—that's how long it lasted with Rod. The exotic places he showed her were second-rate dives and sleazy motels. She couldn't even remember the name of the town where he left her—alone and pregnant. No, never again would she follow a musician.

The melancholy sound of the guitar reached deep into her heart, and Megan sighed. It all seemed so long ago. Rod was now dead and his son was ten years old. But in a way Rod's prediction had been right. From the minute she'd called her father and asked him to come and get her, she'd never felt alone again.

"The dude's not bad," Pete said, when Sam finished the piece. "Will he be taking the Panche kid's place?"

"He's just playing tonight. Tomorrow, who knows where he'll be. You know how these musicians are."

"Too bad. A guy like that's good for business."

"Two beers, screwdriver and a strawberry daiquiri!" Nancy yelled, dropping her tray on the counter and leaning against the bar. "Man, he turns me on," she sighed, watching Sam move across the room to the exit door.

"Can you take over?" Megan asked Pete, her own eyes following Sam's progress. "I have to talk to him about his wages before I leave."

"No problem," Pete assured her, reaching for a bottle of rum.

Megan started for the back door. She knew she didn't really have to talk to Sam about his wages; she could simply go home and tell her father to pay him top dollar. He was worth it just for the extra business he'd brought in. In fact, by meeting him she was doing exactly as Sam wanted. But it seemed she couldn't stop herself.

She pushed open the door and stepped out of the air-conditioned bar. Clouds covered the sky, raising the humidity level and making it dark as midnight. A spotlight mounted on the corner of the building flooded the area around the door, illuminating the dumpster and a patch of grass that ran from the building to the lakeshore. Sam was nowhere to be seen. Then she heard a click and, in a darkened corner away from the door, saw the flicker of a lighter's flame.

"You're good," she said, stepping toward the glow of Sam's cigarette. "Really good. Certainly worth a lot more than we can afford to pay you."

"I told you before, pay me whatever you were going to pay that piano player."

"Who are you, Sam Blake?" she asked, stopping in front of him.

"Just a guitar player."

"You know you're too good to be playing in a bar like ours."

"No one's ever too good to play where people appreciate music." He dropped his cigarette and crushed it out with the toe of his boot. Reaching forward, he touched the side of her face with his fingertips. "Besides, I'm enjoying myself." His fingers moved over the contour of her cheek, and he stepped closer.

Megan's heartbeat increased dramatically. Experience told her to beware, to step back or tell him to stop. Instead she took a deep breath, inhaling the aroma of after-shave and a masculine scent that was distinctly Sam Blake's. She knew she would never forget the combination.

"Have you ever been instantly attracted to someone?" he asked softly, his other hand coming up to cradle her face.

Megan said nothing. He was voicing her own feelings and she didn't know what to say. All she could do was stare at him, her eyes focused on his lips.

"It's not just your looks," he went on, his thumbs lightly tracing over the softness of her cheeks, "though you're a very attractive woman, Megan McGuire." Slowly he lowered his head toward hers.

"Sam, don't," she whispered, but even as she objected, Megan tilted her head back slightly.

His mouth brushed over hers in a manner far more gentle and hesitant than she'd expected. The brief contact set her pulse racing, and it took all of her willpower not to reach out and touch him. Instead, she closed her eyes and tried to block out the delightfully erotic sensations he was arousing.

"I've wanted to kiss you ever since I first saw you," he murmured, his hands moving to the back of her head to gently massage her neck.

"I should go back inside," Megan mumbled, not making a move to leave.

"Why?" He kissed her again, his lips leisurely playing over hers.

It was impossible to ignore the feelings he was awakening. She wanted to respond, to taste, to hold, to—"No!" Megan gasped, pushing against his chest with her palms. "You've got to stop this." She stepped back, hoping to free herself from the control he seemed to have over her.

"What are you afraid of, Megan?" he asked softly, his hands dropping to her shoulders to stop her retreat.

"Nothing. I . . . I just don't want you to kiss me." She didn't dare let him know how good his lips had felt on hers.

"I think you do."

"Then you're wrong." Boldly she looked up at him.

"Am I?"

"Yes, you are."

He said nothing in reply. Instead his thumbs continued to make small circular motions along the sides of her neck.

Megan knew that the rapid throb of her pulse was telling him exactly how he affected her.

Her body having thus betrayed her, she tried a different approach. "Look, let's be sensible. I don't have time to get involved with anyone."

His hands slid down to her arms, his fingers lightly caressing her soft skin. "You know what they say about all work and no play."

His were gentle fingers, graceful fingers. Just as he'd stroked his guitar and brought forth beautiful music, he was stroking her, bringing forth exquisite pleasure, and for a moment she forgot everything but his touch. Then reason prevailed once more. "It couldn't lead anywhere."

"Just where do you want it to lead?"

"Nowhere." She was trembling ever so slightly, her heart beating wildly.

Gently he slid his arms around her. "It would be good between us, Megan. I'm sure of that."

Breathless, she could hardly speak. "I don't want to get involved with you," she whispered, her stomach reacting strangely as he tightened his grip and drew her closer to his lean, hard body.

"I want to get involved with you."

He was so positive, so certain, that it frightened her. "Sam, I—"

The rest of her sentence was swallowed by his kiss, his mouth taking total possession of hers. She tried to remain passive, stay stiff in his arms and pretend she wasn't involved. But with their bodies pressed so tightly—curve against angle, soft molded to hard—indifference was impossible.

She knew if she struggled he would let her go, but Megan discovered she didn't really want to be free of Sam Blake's embrace. She liked the feel of his arms around her, the way their bodies fitted together, and she liked the taste of his mouth. Giving in, she reached out and wrapped her arms around his rib cage, pressing her fingers into his back. Beneath her palms she could feel the smooth play of his muscles and the heat of his body. Her mouth became pliant, moving with his, blending with his, and when his tongue darted out to tease and prod, she willingly parted her lips to give him entry to the moist, warm inner sanctum.

All the while he kissed her, his hands traveled over her back, seductively caressing her shoulders, her neck and her spine. The fire in her loins spread throughout her body, warming her flesh and weakening her limbs. Curling her fingers into his shirt, like a cat kneading a blanket, she groaned in pleasure.

"Megan." He murmured her name almost reverently, lifting his mouth from hers to gaze down at her flushed face.

Confused by the emotions she was experiencing, she could only utter his name, her hands moving up to his hair. It was soft hair, thick twisting curls that beckoned her touch. She combed her fingers into its mass and closed her eyes, letting her head fall back. He kissed her throat, his tongue darting out to wet the sensitive hollow at the base of her neck, and she automatically arched against him, leaning on his arm for support.

His breathing was rapid, the hard lines of his body telling her of his growing desire. It excited her to know she could arouse him. That she herself could feel such a burning need excited and frightened her.

With a firm pressure of his hands he lifted her to her toes, and Megan was molded against his length. She knew that he wanted to make love to her, yet he was maintaining a tight rein on his desires. His only aggressive act was the intimate exploration of her mouth with his tongue. Time lost all meaning and when the exit door to the bar opened, the noise from inside flowing out in a great rush, Megan jerked back in surprise.

Sam stopped her retreat, a finger placed quickly against her lips silencing any comment as he drew her farther into the shadows. With her back to the door, it was impossible for her to see who had come out of the bar. Clinging to Sam, afraid to even breathe, Megan listened.

The peacefulness of the night was shattered by the curses of a man. It was obvious from the slurred words that their visitor had had more than enough to drink and had missed the door to the men's room. Everyone, especially the architect of the building, was being cussed out for poor planning.

Clinging to Sam, Megan listened to the sound of unsteady footsteps on gravel and then the door being opened again. As the noise from inside increased, then became muffled as the door closed, she laughed self-consciously. "I thought for sure he'd see us."

"He had other things on his mind."

"Sam?" She stared at him, wondering why it felt so right to be held by a man she barely knew.

"What?" Lightly he kissed her lips.

One thing the drunk had succeeded in doing was bringing her to her senses. Megan pulled back. "I don't know what just came over me. I may work in a bar, but I'm not the sort of woman who lets a man pick her up and then—"

"I know." Sam leaned forward to kiss her again.

"No." Quickly she turned her head. "I've got to go, and so do you." She was afraid it wouldn't take long for him to rekindle the flame he'd so easily ignited. "It has to be past ten. The customers will be expecting you to play again."

"They'll wait." Leaning close, he nipped her earlobe and caught the tiny knob of her gold earring.

"I've got to get home. My son's expecting me." The thought of Josh reminded her that Sam was one man she definitely did not want to get involved with. Megan wriggled to free herself from his hold.

He let her go and watched her back away, then sighed. "All right, slave driver, I'll get back to work."

"I want you to know I appreciate your helping us out tonight."

"My pleasure."

"And I've enjoyed meeting you . . . and listening to your music."

"Enjoyed meeting me?" He chuckled. "I think, my dear, that we've done a lot more than just meet. I'd say we've taken the first steps toward a *very* close relationship."

Shocked by his words, Megan backed up even farther, raising her hands in front of her, as if to stop him should he try to touch her. "Look, Sam, I'll admit I find you attractive. And I love the way you play the guitar. I won't even deny that I enjoyed being kissed by you, but I've said it before and I mean it. I'm not getting involved with a guitar player."

"I think you are."

"Then you're wrong."

"You're going to turn your back on your feelings, simply because I'm a musician?" He frowned and reached into his pocket for a cigarette.

"You'll be late for your next set if you smoke that," Megan said quickly.

"So, fire me."

In the light of the flame from his lighter she could see his face clearly. His blue eyes were focused on her, his sensual mouth set in a firm line, his square jaw rigid. He looked angry and she felt guilty.

"Sam, I'm sorry. I never should have come out here. I'm sure it seemed as if . . ."

He said nothing, his gaze never wavering.

"Maybe I'm wrong to . . . to feel the way I do," she stammered. "If you knew . . ." But once again she couldn't finish. Taking a deep breath, Megan forced herself to act composed. "Actually, right now I don't have time to get involved with anyone." She turned away and took a few steps toward the door, then stopped and faced him again. "I have to go home. It's time for Dad to come on duty, and I have to be there for Josh."

Still he said nothing.

"Thanks again for helping us out tonight. Dad will pay you." Closing her eyes, she whispered, "Goodbye, Sam."

It was then he smiled. "Good night, Megan."

3

MEGAN WAS LATE getting home. She apologized to her dad without really explaining what had held her up, assured him that Sam Blake was not just a good guitar player but fantastic, and gave him a quick kiss before he left for his shift. Then she tried to act as if nothing had happened, as if Sam had not held her in his arms and kissed her.

Josh and she made popcorn, sat together on the couch and watched television. But her mind wasn't on the car chases and shoot-outs flashing across the screen. As hard as she tried to block him out, her thoughts kept returning to one blond guitar player.

What was there about the man that made him so attractive, she wondered. She'd been a fool to meet him out back. She'd done exactly what he'd asked—virtually walked into his arms. No wonder he'd thought he could kiss her. She, however, hadn't expected it. Nor had she expected to like his kisses so much. Why, oh, why was he a musician?

At eleven she put Josh to bed, did the few dishes in the sink and headed for bed, too, telling herself that he'd be gone tomorrow. She should just forget him. But Megan discovered she couldn't do that. And she couldn't sleep. Whenever she closed her eyes, she saw images of Sam playing his guitar, his fingers flying over the strings.

Her opinion of the guitar had never been overly flattering. Anyone could play it, she'd always thought. Even she could strum a few basic chords that Rod had taught her. Yet the music she'd heard that evening had been so different from anything Rod had ever played. And Sam seemed different.

Megan rolled to her side and bunched her pillow beneath her head. Not since Rod had a man captured her interest so quickly. Perhaps she had a strange penchant for musicians. Or maybe it was just Sam Blake's looks that had attracted her.

He certainly couldn't be called handsome. Interesting, yes. Intriguing. But not handsome. His was a face with character. A face she would love to draw, she thought, not for the first time.

Drawing had always been her way of expressing her feelings. But then, she supposed it was probably natural for the daughter of an art teacher to find emotional release through painting and sketching. She longed to get back to her artwork. It had been weeks since she'd done any painting; the bar was taking up too much of her time and energy.

That's how she would get him out of her system, she decided. She would draw him. Analyzed, fantasy would give way to reason. She would capture Sam Blake on paper and purge him from her thoughts. Megan left her bed to find her drawing tablet and pencils. Sitting in the rocking chair by her window, she began to sketch.

Simple curling lines became his hair; a jagged, angular line the contour of his face. Closing her eyes, she could picture Sam leaning over his guitar. Quickly her pencil skimmed over the paper. She exaggerated the length of his fingers and used thick, straight lines to represent the strings of the guitar. Not satisfied, she dropped the drawing on the floor and started another.

She drew him sitting on the stool, his left leg higher than his right, the guitar forming a strong diagonal. This time she sketched in every detail she could remember—the buckles on his boots, the clean lines of his trousers and the way he left the top buttons of his shirt open, exposing the hairs on his chest. When she began to work on his face, the shape and curve of his lips captured her complete attention. How well she remembered those lips—the top a little on the thin side, with just a bit of a dip in the center . . . but not too much. The bottom curve fuller. Warm, sensual lips that had felt so good against hers. Her hand shook and the line was ruined.

By three o'clock, five drawings of Sam lay on the floor, and Megan was physically drained. Standing, she studied all five and wasn't satisfied with any of them. But the exercise had helped. When she returned to her bed she was too tired to wonder why she'd reacted as she had. Closing her eyes, she fell into a deep sleep, not even stirring when her father arrived home after four—humming.

THE SOUND OF THE TELEVISION SET going in the living room told Megan that Josh was up. Then she could hear him in the kitchen: the clatter of a bowl being taken from the cupboard, the rustling of a box being opened, the opening and closing of the refrigerator and, finally, the clink of a spoon. Another cereal morning. Megan looked at the clock at her bedside and groaned. Nine o'clock. She'd planned on getting up early and fixing her son pancakes and eggs. It was too late now.

Rising slowly, Megan wondered why she felt so tired, then, seeing the drawings on the floor by the chair, remembered. "You'd already forgotten him," she muttered, laughing at herself, satisfied that her hours of drawing had been beneficial.

A quick shower refreshed her, then she donned white shorts and a red T-shirt. She relished the morning hours, when she could be cool and comfortable. Later, that afternoon, she would have to put on her uniform and once again play the role of barkeeper.

Dressed, her short hair nearly dry, she picked up the sketches of Sam and his guitar and stuffed them into a folder. "Out of sight, out of mind, Mr. Blake," she insisted, placing the folder on a shelf and leaving the bedroom.

With a radiant smile, she strolled into the living room, where her son was sprawled in front of the television set, an empty bowl of cereal by his side. "'Morning, Josh," she greeted him, leaning over to ruffle a head of thick, brown hair.

He looked up, his eyes a startling shade of deep blue. "Hi. Boy, you and Grampa sure are lazy. I even had to get my own breakfast."

He grumbled the words and nodded abruptly toward the empty cereal bowl, but Megan detected a look of pride on her son's face. Lately he'd become more and more independent. "I was up late last night. Drawing," she explained. "And Grampa came in after three, so he's probably very tired. Did you get enough to eat?"

"Yeah." Josh's attention was caught by the action on the television screen.

Megan wandered into the kitchen, wiped up some spilled milk and started a pot of coffee. A piece of toast and a glass of orange juice sufficed as breakfast, followed by a steaming cup of coffee. She peeked in on her father once, concerned. Herb McGuire wasn't one to sleep in late. Hearing his loud, resonant snores, she decided all was well.

"I've got to do some grocery shopping. Want to come along?" Megan asked Josh.

He watched her buckle her sandals and weighed the possibility of getting a treat if he went along against missing the show he was watching. Finally he shook his head but ventured, "Buy me some gum, Mom. Please?"

"What kind?" She searched for her purse and found it next to the easy chair, where she'd dropped it the night before.

"Wammy Wacko." Josh gave her a wistful look.

"Wammy Wacko? What will they think of next." Megan leaned down and dropped a kiss on his forehead, then paused to accept the hug he gave her in return. "If Grampa's not up by ten, you'd better wake him," she said, opening the back door.

It was going to be another hot day, but overnight the sky had cleared and a slight breeze eased the humidity. Megan paused for a moment to look across the lake. All along the shoreline, nestled amid pines, were year-round homes and summer cottages. On the water, sailboats, bass boats, dinghies and pontoons bobbed and pulled at their moorings. Several children were already outside, swimming and playing.

Shady Lake wasn't a large lake—the opposite shoreline easily visible until it curved around a bend—but its appeal was its excellent fishing, sandy beaches and good swimming. Though many families came to Shady Lake for vacations, many lived there year-round.

Megan and her father thought they'd had an enormous stroke of good luck, when they'd seen the ad: "For sale. Resort bar. Good business. Owner must sell because of illness." Shady Lake had sounded like the perfect location for a bar.

They hadn't known then that they'd have stiff competition or that they'd have so much trouble getting entertainers. They'd thought they were getting a bargain. Now she wondered.

The best aspect of their move from Grand Rapids had been the house they were renting. It was right on the lake so Josh could swim and fish in the summer, ice skate and ice fish in the winter. And, if not exactly a mansion, the house was spacious enough for the three of them. At least they each had a bedroom, and the kitchen had been modernized. There was even a guest cottage that Megan had immediately transformed into an art studio. Unfortunately she hadn't found time to use it as much as she would have liked.

Taking in a deep, refreshing breath of morning air, Megan turned and walked toward the garage. Parked on the grassy strip that separated their property from the neighbor's was a black Porsche. "Classy," she murmured, eyeing the sleek car. Mrs. Vitteck's taste in boyfriends was definitely improving. Even so, Megan wished her neighbor would tell her guests to park on her side of the property line.

Megan opened her garage door. Eight years old, rusted and inclined to refuse to start on cold mornings, the yellow Volkswagen inside was practically a member of the family. An economical member. She backed out carefully, not wanting to think what it would cost to repair a dent or scratch on the ebony finish of the Porsche.

From her house it was only a mile to Shady Lake's business district, closer by way of the path along the lake. Within minutes she was pulling up in front of the grocery store, which was two shops down from The Quarter Note. Wide aisles and friendly employees made shopping a pleasure, and Megan would have finished quickly if she hadn't been stopped just before the checkout stand by Nancy.

"Find out what was wrong with the lights?" the blond waitress asked, looking only half awake. She pushed her nearly empty cart up next to Megan's.

"I didn't know there was anything wrong with them." Megan looked at the eggs and bacon in Nancy's cart and caught herself wondering if Sam Blake had ended up going home with the attractive waitress. Was this to be a brunch for two? Immediately she squelched the thought. "What happened?"

"Last night, about midnight, all the lights in the place went out. Kaput. Nothing." Nancy laughed. "I didn't know there were so many men with wandering hands. Why, ah barely escaped with mah virtue."

"Were the lights out long?" asked Megan, ignoring Nancy's feigned Southern drawl and concern for her questionable virtue.

"About five minutes. Your dad reset the fuses and the lights were fine after that, but he and that guitar player stayed after to check it out. I was wondering if they found anything?"

So Sam hadn't gone home with her. For reasons Megan didn't like to admit to herself, she felt relieved. "Dad was still asleep when I left this morning. I don't know."

"So what do you think of that guy?" Nancy asked, her penciled eyebrows lifting curiously.

"What guy?" Megan tried to look disinterested by checking over her shopping list.

"That guitar player." Nancy gave her a light poke on the arm. "Is he a good kisser?"

"I don't know what you're talking about." She could feel the color rising to her cheeks and tried to control it. Somewhere along the line Nancy had never learned the proper respect for her employers. Or maybe it was her fault. She was too friendly with her employees.

"You two were certainly out back a long time." Nancy grinned knowingly.

"We were discussing his wages."

"Fringe benefits would be more like it. Next time don't forget to blot your lipstick before you start negotiations."

No effort on her part could now keep the telltale blush from Megan's cheeks. "We...that is...I..."

Nancy couldn't stop laughing. "I think he must have been pretty good." Still laughing, she pushed her cart away.

MEGAN EASED her car past the black Porsche and into the garage. As she carried the two grocery sacks and balanced a gallon of milk in the crook of her arm, the first thing she noticed when she entered the house was the quiet. She was just beginning to wonder where everyone was when the telephone rang. Setting the groceries on the kitchen table, she grabbed for the receiver.

"About time you got home," her father lightly chastised.

"About time you got up," she responded, "Where are you?"

"At the bar. The burglar alarm went off, so the sheriff called. Must have been a loose wire. I think I'll stick around and see if I can find the problem."

"I saw Nancy at the grocery store. She said you had trouble with the lights last night." Megan was relieved that there hadn't been a break-in. Cradling the receiver on her shoulder, she began to put away the groceries, talking to her father as she worked. "We should have the place re-wired."

"You know we can't afford it right now."

"Is it safe not to?"

"As soon as business picks up," he promised, ignoring her question.

"Right." It was becoming an empty promise, yet she didn't know any alternative. They were extended to their limits. "Ask Josh if he still wants to go swimming."

"Josh isn't here. I didn't know what I might find, so I left him with Sam."

"Sam?" questioned Megan, her hand stopping in mid-air, in the act of lifting a can of soup toward the cupboard.

"Sam Blake. Our guitar player," her father answered matter-of-factly. "He's in the guest cabin. He couldn't find a place to stay last night, so I told him he might as well use ours. No one else ever does."

"But that's my studio," Megan cried, the soup can slipping from her hand and dropping to the floor.

"It also has a bed and a couch. It seemed senseless for him to rent a place when we had one available."

Quickly she picked up the can and put it away. Sam Blake was still around. The car. The black Porsche. It was his. He was here, only a few yards away, and he had her son with him. "Dad, I've got to go." She hurriedly shoved the last of the perishables into the refrigerator. "I'll see you later."

Megan ran the short distance between the house and the simple two-room guest cabin. Her heart was in her throat as she knocked on the screen door. From inside she could hear the hesitant plucking of a guitar and closed her eyes. She knew what that sound meant.

From the time her son had been old enough to ask, she'd told him about his father, keeping it as simple as she could. She'd explained that Rod had been a musician, that he'd played with a band and that he'd died in a car crash. And one day, after a cruel schoolmate teased her son, she'd explained what the word "bastard" meant.

Josh had accepted everything, never knowing his father hadn't wanted him. Lately, however, he'd been begging to be in the sixth grade band and to take piano lessons. Both requests she'd been able to put off. She'd told him they couldn't afford to rent or buy an instrument right now and that she didn't want him using the piano at the bar. How long those excuses would last, she didn't know.

Megan heard footsteps and opened her eyes. She wasn't ready for this confrontation. Seeing Sam through the screen door, she could feel the magnetism and was more aware than ever that her drawings hadn't begun to capture the essence of this man.

He was wearing only a pair of denim cutoffs, curly blond hairs forming a pale covering across his chest then thinning to a V that ended somewhere beyond a leather belt. Though not overly muscular, his body was lean and trim, his appearance totally male and totally disconcerting. Involuntarily she took in a breath as he opened the door. "Hi," he said softly, the low tone of his voice seductively alluring.

She didn't like the way her pulse took off or that butterflies suddenly invaded her stomach. Staring at him, her mouth open, she couldn't think of a word to say.

"I imagine you're looking for your son," he supplied, stepping back in an unspoken invitation for her to come inside.

"Yes." She hesitated, wondering if she couldn't just stay where she was and yell for Josh. She could see him in the kitchenette, seated on a chair, a guitar across his lap. Megan decided against yelling. Knowing her son, she was certain he wouldn't leave that guitar without a fuss. Head held high, a forced smile on her lips, she stepped past Sam and walked directly toward Josh.

"Hi, Mom," he said, beaming with excitement. "Sam's teaching me 'Skip to My Lou.' Listen." He pressed two left fingers against the neck of the guitar and with the thumb and two fingers of his right hand plucked four strings in a pattern that sounded vaguely similar to the song she knew.

Megan involuntarily tensed as she watched her son play. Seeing Josh's head bent over the guitar, his long, brown bangs falling across his forehead, brought back memories of his father. Too many memories. "That's enough!" she snapped, grabbing the guitar from his hands before he realized what she was doing. "I've told you before, I don't want you playing the guitar!"

"But, Mom." Josh stared at her wide-eyed, surprised by her anger.

"No buts." She handed the guitar to Sam. "Now say goodbye to Mr. Blake. We're leaving."

"But he promised he would teach me to play 'Blue-Tail Fly.'" Tears were forming in the boy's eyes. He looked first at his mother, then at Sam, his expression a plea for help.

"Not now," Sam answered quietly.

"Later?" Josh asked hopefully.

"Mr. Blake won't be here later." Megan interrupted. She faced Sam squarely, tilting her chin up to look at him. "Will you?"

Sam motioned with his hand for Josh to leave. For a moment the boy paused, undecided, then hurried toward the door. Neither Sam nor Megan said a word until the screen door slammed shut and Josh was on his way to the main house.

"You *are* leaving, aren't you?" she asked, afraid she already knew the answer.

"Someday." He stepped away from her to carry the guitar over to its case. Carefully he put it away and snapped the lid shut.

"But what about Cash Barrigan? You were following him. You wanted to learn some songs he knew." She wanted desperately for him to say he was going, that he would soon be out of her life—and away from her son.

Sam straightened, turned and smiled at her. "I have enough songs. I'll catch up with Cash another time. Your Dad offered me a job last night. I told him I'd stay for a while."

"No . . ." She let the word out in an extended gasp. Closing her eyes, Megan turned her back to him and tried to understand what was happening. He could not stay. She didn't want him teaching her son how to play the guitar— she didn't want him confusing her life with his crazy appeal.

"Megan," he said softly, his hands touching her shoulders.

She jumped, unaware that he'd come up behind her. The warmth of his hands brought back memories of the night before—of the feel of his body against hers, so alive and hard. She trembled.

He felt her body quiver and the urge to turn her around and gather her into his arms was overpowering. But he resisted. She was afraid of him. Why, he wasn't certain, but he knew he would have to take it slowly. "Last night your dad said the bar was in financial trouble. I want to help, if I can."

His voice was hypnotic, his slight accent a delight. Everything about him seemed so familiar—his smell, his touch. She nearly leaned back against him, then caught herself. "No," she groaned and pulled away. Shakily she walked over to the open window that looked out across the lake, took in a deep breath of fresh air and slowly expelled it. "We don't need your help."

"Don't you?" He watched her for a moment, then moved to the kitchenette.

When he struck a match, she turned to watch him light a cigarette. "Dad should have asked me first, before he offered you a job. We're partners. He should have asked."

Sam shook out the match, his eyes meshing with hers. "What are you afraid of, Megan?"

His question caught her off guard. "I'm not afraid. It's just that I...you..." She couldn't tell him. And she couldn't think of one good reason why he shouldn't play at The Quarter Note. In fact, he was right—they did need his help. "Well, I know you won't stay long, so if you want to work at the bar, fine. But you can't stay here. This is my studio. This is where I do my drawing and painting."

"I noticed your work." He pointed toward the easel he'd pushed over to the corner, along with the large cardboard portfolio by its side. "You're quite good."

"You sound surprised."

"I suppose I am. It isn't every day I meet a barkeeper who also draws and paints."

"I was a free-lance illustrator before I became a bar owner. And as soon as we get The Quarter Note on its feet, I'll be a free-lance illustrator again."

"So let's get that bar on its feet." He smiled. "And while I'm here, I might want to hire you."

"For what?" she asked suspiciously.

"An album cover. I don't know. Maybe a drawing of me playing the guitar. What do you think?"

"An album cover?"

"Yes. I want to record some of these folk songs I've been learning."

"Why? So you can reach stardom? Be on the pop charts?" Her attitude was clearly sarcastic. That had always been Rod's dream. A dream he never knew had eventually come true.

Sam laughed. "I doubt if that would ever happen. No, this is just a pet project of mine."

A pet project. Well, if he could drive a Porsche, he could probably afford pet projects like record albums. She, however, had more pressing concerns. "Sorry, but I can't."

"All I'm looking for is a black-and-white drawing of me playing the guitar. Something stylized. You could probably do it in a few hours." He drew on his cigarette and watched the expression on her face.

His words reminded her of the drawings she'd done early that morning, when sleep had eluded her and the feel of his kisses still lingered on her lips. For a moment she wondered if he could have possibly seen those sketches. But no, they were in the folder in her bedroom.

White smoke rose slowly above his head. He didn't move, his blue eyes locked with hers. "What do you think? Are you game?"

She knew the drawings in her bedroom wouldn't do. In them she'd failed to capture the vibrancy he radiated. No, to do the kind of drawing he was suggesting, she would have to have him in front of her, playing the guitar. Maybe then she could catch the spirit of his character. But that would mean she'd have to spend time with him, and *that* she didn't want to do. "I can't," she said.

"I'll pay you, if that's what you're worried about."

She shook her head. "It's not the money. I just don't have the time."

"You don't have time to draw me?" he asked, cocking his head slightly to the side, his eyebrows rising.

Again she shook her head. "I haven't had time to do any painting or drawing for weeks."

A satisfied smile curved his lips. "That's what your father said. And if you're not using this place, my staying here shouldn't be a problem. Right?"

He'd tricked her, Megan realized. He'd gotten her to say exactly what he wanted, to confess that she wasn't using the studio. She could have kicked herself for being so gullible. No, she'd rather kick him. "You probably aren't even planning on making an album," she snapped. "Well, you can take your bag of tricks and get out of here, Mr. Blake. I don't need any excuses. I just plain don't want you around." Angry, she headed for the door.

Immediately Sam put out his cigarette and started after her. His long legs covered the distance quickly, and he caught her before she opened the screen. Grabbing her by the shoulders, he turned her to face him. "I am going to record an album. And I liked the portraits I saw in your portfolio. And furthermore, I think your style might be just what I've been looking for." His blue eyes were dark, his features unyielding as he stared down at her. Then he took a deep, relaxing breath and loosened his hold a bit. "All right, maybe I did try to trick you. Your father and I had a long friendly talk last night. I like the man. And if my playing at The Quarter Note would help, I'm more than willing to stick around here for a while. Your father graciously offered me the use of this cabin. Now, can you give me one good, logical reason why I shouldn't?"

"I don't want Josh associating with you," she blurted before thinking.

"Why?" Sam stiffened and let go of her arms.

Raising her chin, Megan looked him squarely in the eyes. "Because I don't want my son playing the guitar. I don't want Josh to learn how to play any instrument."

"And what about what Josh wants?" Sam frowned. "I wasn't the one who asked him to play. He was the one who wanted to see my guitar, who begged to touch it and play it."

"Because right now he thinks playing a musical instrument is what he wants to do. He'll outgrow it."

"Will he?"

Megan wished she could say yes. From the day Josh realized a rattle could produce a sound he'd been abnormally fascinated by anything that made noise. For ten years she'd encouraged her son to be active in sports, to read, to draw . . . to do anything but play an instrument. Seeing Josh with a guitar, she couldn't help thinking that her efforts had been futile. "I don't want my son to become so obsessed with music and the need for fame that he'll step on anyone who gets in his way."

"And who says it has to be that way?" challenged Sam.

"I do," snapped Megan. "Because I know whose son he is."

For a moment neither of them said anything. The tension in the air was tangible. It was Sam who first spoke, his voice low. "His father was a musician?"

"Yes."

"You're divorced?"

"We were never married." She saw no reason to lie. If her father hadn't already told Sam, someone else would.

"And this man, Josh's father, he hurt you?"

Megan laughed sarcastically. "He hurt everyone." Then she sobered. "If you don't mind, I'd rather not talk about him."

He wanted to ask more, but held back. "Megan," he said finally, "no matter what your feelings are for your son's father, Josh is musically gifted. I've never seen anyone pick up a guitar and start playing the way he did today. He couldn't absorb what I was telling him fast enough."

"No," she protested, shaking her head. She didn't want to hear those words.

"Yes. And denying it isn't going to make it go away."

"No, no, no!" she cried, her eyes pleading with him to take back what he'd said.

"Megan, you can't stop him from being who he is."

Sam reached for her, but she stepped back, bumping against the screen door. "Maybe not, but I'm going to try."

She looked at the guitar case by the couch and wished she could break it into a million pieces. If only Sam Blake had never walked into their lives. But he had. And, if she knew her Irish father's stubborn streak, Sam Blake was probably going to stay—right in this cabin.

Adopting a calm she didn't truly feel, she looked back at Sam. "You've got to make me one promise. As long as you're here in this guest cabin, you will not let Josh play the guitar. You won't let him even touch it. Do you promise?"

"You're making a mistake," he said. "Maybe you can keep Josh from doing what he wants for a little while, but one day he'll break away from you. And when he does, you'll lose him."

"I'll take that chance," she retorted. "Now, do I have your promise?"

He wanted to tell her that he knew how Josh felt, that she couldn't stop the boy, even if she wanted to. But he knew she wouldn't listen. No more than his own mother had listened to him. "You have my promise," he said reluctantly. "At least until I change your mind."

"That you won't do," she said, a feeling of relief flooding over her. "Now I have to go talk to Josh." Turning on her heel, she shoved the screen door open and left the cabin.

"HOW COULD YOU hire him, without even asking me?" Megan asked her father, who was changing fuses in the outdated electrical box by the dumpster.

"How?" Her father glanced her way, grinning. "Easy enough. I just asked him. As for asking you, I didn't think you'd object. The guy's great."

"But to offer him our guest cabin?" That just wasn't like her father.

"We're not using it. You haven't been out there for weeks. Why not let him use it?"

"Dad, I don't like the idea of him being around Josh."

Her father stopped twisting a fuse to study her. "What's really bothering you, Meg?"

She sighed. "He was teaching Josh how to play the guitar this morning. You know how I feel about that."

"You're not going to be able to keep that boy away from music forever."

She turned her head to look down by the water's edge, where Josh was tossing stones. One by one the rocks splashed into the murky blue-green water. Josh was still sulking because she'd told him he couldn't play Sam's guitar. She'd told him, truthfully, that if anything happened to that guitar, they couldn't afford to replace it.

Josh hadn't liked her edict any more than Megan now liked hearing her father voice almost the same words Sam had. "I've got to try, Dad," she insisted. "You don't want Josh to turn out like his father, do you?"

Herb's gaze returned to his daughter's face. "You mean, do I want my grandson to leave some disillusioned girl alone and pregnant? Honey, Josh isn't like Rod. And neither is Sam."

"How do you know that? In fact, just exactly what do we know about Sam Blake?"

"He's a nice guy." Herb grinned and wiped his arm across his damp forehead. "I like the way he talks. Sort of like Cary Grant."

"Oh, great!" Sam had everyone mesmerized. Even her dad. "You like him because he sounds like a movie actor. Dad, an accent doesn't make someone a nice guy."

"Maybe not, but he stayed after and helped me last night. That counts for something. And he's obviously very talented."

"Right. And did you know he drives a Porsche? A very black, very sleek and very expensive Porsche?"

"He followed me home in it. So the man likes to drive a nice car. I didn't realize that qualified as a character flaw."

Megan glared at her father. He was being unduly obstinate. "It's not a character flaw, but obviously Sam has money. Lots of money. As well as talent. So why is he willing to play here, at The Quarter Note? We barely pay above minimum, and Shady Lake certainly can't be considered the hub of the entertainment world."

Herb finished changing the fuses and snapped the metal door shut. Tossing the old fuses into the dumpster, he turned to face his daughter. "Maybe Sam Blake doesn't need to be in the center of the entertainment world."

"Ha!" scoffed Megan. "You forget, I know musicians. They all want to be in the limelight. It's in their blood." She looked at her son and wished that wasn't true.

"Maybe that's not true of all musicians," her father said softly, knowing her concern.

4

IT WAS INCREDIBLE how quickly word spread of the new guitar player at The Quarter Note. Saturday afternoon Megan spent as much time answering the telephone—telling people Sam Blake would be playing again that night—as she did mixing drinks. And by eight o'clock the place was filling rapidly. When Sam arrived at eight forty-five, there were only three empty tables, a phenomenon The Quarter Note hadn't experienced since the first week of their opening.

Once again he was dressed all in black, and Megan felt a strange, quivering sensation invade her insides the moment he stepped through the door, guitar case in hand. He looked her way and smiled. She pretended she was busy with an order, but out of the corner of her eye she watched him. He greeted patrons congenially as he passed their tables on the way to the platform, sometimes stopping to shake hands, accept a personal request for a song or say a few words. He was relaxed, completely at ease. Megan felt as tense as an overly tightened string.

He made no attempt to talk to her, and for that she was thankful. She was tired from too few hours of sleep and on edge from arguing with her son. Sam had given Josh a taste of playing the guitar and the boy wanted more. To make matters worse, her father was actually siding with Josh. At the moment she would have gladly told Sam

Blake where he could take his guitar. And what he could do with it.

For forty-five minutes he played and she fixed drinks. It was a pleasure to be busy, but it was also tiring and she was glad when her shift was over. As Sam finished his first set, she slipped out of The Quarter Note, the sound of applause still ringing in her ears. That the customers liked him was evident, and for some foolish reason, that made her even more irritable.

"Why don't you go away, Sam Blake," Megan muttered to herself, as she drove the short distance to the house. "Take off. I won't even blame you for walking out on us. Just go."

Maybe financially they needed him at The Quarter Note, but she certainly didn't need him tempting Josh with ideas about playing the guitar. Perhaps she couldn't stop her son from someday playing a musical instrument, but she certainly intended to put him off for as long as she could.

And there was another reason she wanted Sam to leave. She was uneasy with the feelings she experienced whenever he was near. Or when he'd kissed her. Of course, it had been a year since she'd been romantically involved with a man...eleven years since she'd slept with one. And she would be twenty-nine in three months. That was it. A woman at the height of her sexuality.

"Great timing," she mumbled, and pulled into the drive going a bit too fast. It seemed even her hormones were plotting against her. "Well, body, you can forget it," she muttered. "I don't have time to get involved with a man— least of all a musician." Nevertheless, for her own sanity she decided she would steer clear of Sam Blake as much as possible.

On Sunday Megan took Josh to church and then to the John Ball Park Zoo in Grand Rapids. For twenty-four hours she'd managed to avoid seeing Sam. But a little after midnight, their regular Sunday closing time, Sam and her father arrived home together. She was in bed when the sound of voices and car doors slamming alerted her to their arrival. "Best crowd we've ever had on a Sunday night," Megan heard her father say.

The crunch of footsteps on gravel stopped outside her bedroom window. She blinked open her eyes and saw two silhouettes through the shade—one tall and lean, the other slightly shorter and bulkier. Her father sucked in a deep breath of night air and let it out with a weary sigh. "Can't tell you how much I appreciate your staying on like this, Sam."

"I'm enjoying myself."

"We usually have a pretty small crowd on Monday nights, but would you mind playing from eight to ten?"

"Not at all. Maybe your daughter would walk me home."

They both laughed and Megan sat up in bed, glaring into the darkness.

"About my daughter..."

Sam was still laughing. "Don't worry about Megan."

Holding her breath, she strained to hear their words.

"She can be very stubborn."

"So can I. 'Night, Herb." The tall, lean shadow started toward the guest cabin.

Then she heard the back door of the house open and close. Sliding out of bed, Megan reached for her robe. "So your daughter's stubborn, is she?" she repeated curtly, coming up behind her father in the kitchen.

"You still up?" Herb turned from the sink, where he was washing his hands. Her frown stopped his smile.

"What were you and Sam talking about? Laughing about?"

"Nosy." Her father ignored her anger and affectionately tweaked her nose, his hand still wet. Then he reached for a towel.

"Dad!" Megan glowered at him.

"I see you're in a good mood." Herb chuckled, then gave her his full attention. "We were discussing Josh. Honey, this would really be an excellent opportunity for him to learn to play the guitar. He's not going to find a better teacher than Sam."

"Josh is not going to learn how to play the guitar," she declared. "And that's that!" She turned abruptly and stalked back to her room.

WHEN JOSH CAME rushing into The Quarter Note Monday afternoon, all excited, Megan was certain it had something to do with the guitar. Lately it seemed as if Josh couldn't talk about anything else.

"I ran all the way," he panted, hopping up on a bar stool. "Please say yes."

"Yes to what?" Megan wasn't that foolish.

"That we can go. It'll be so much fun. And Sam said we can ride in his car, so you won't have to drive at night and we won't be alone and we'll be safe. He says he hasn't seen any for years. And you promised if we could we would, and I—"

"Whoa, whoa." Megan held up the bar mop to signal a stop. "Slow down. Now start over again. What did I promise we would do?"

"Go to Grand Rapids and see the fireworks. Can I have a Coke?" Josh licked his lips thirstily. "I know you said it isn't safe for us to go alone, and that you don't like to drive so far when it's dark, but, see, if Sam takes us you won't have to drive and he can protect us. Please . . ."

Megan poured a glass of Coke and handed it to her son. "I don't think so," she began.

"Why not?" asked her father from the back of the room, where he was working on a chair with a broken rung. "Sounds like a good idea to me. And I do remember you told Josh you might take him."

"Right." Josh's face broke into a wide grin, and he turned on his stool to look at his grandfather. Then his attention returned to his mother. "Please, Mom. We missed them last year. And the year before that because I had the chicken pox. Sam said we could go in early and get a hamburger and stay as late as we wanted."

"Did he send you down here?" Megan wondered just what trickery Sam was up to this time.

"No. But he said I'd have to ask you first. So I came right away. Can we? Please. Please."

"I'll think about it." That was all she would commit herself to. "What about Mrs. Arnosky? Does she know you're here?"

"I don't know," Josh mumbled under his breath and slouched on the stool.

"Did you tell her?"

"No."

"In that case, you get right back home before she starts worrying." If Megan wasn't mistaken, Mrs. Arnosky was probably watching her soap operas and didn't even know Josh was gone. A ten-year-old was really more than the older woman could cope with, but Mrs. Arnosky had been the best to apply for the job. Around Shady Lake good baby-sitters were as scarce as good musicians.

"But can we go with Sam to see the fireworks?" Josh persisted.

"We'll see," she said, hoping something would come up that would give her an excuse for not going. She really didn't want to disappoint her son, but spending an evening with Sam didn't make good sense, either. "I'll have to talk to Mr. Blake first."

"When?" begged Josh.

"Soon."

She wasn't about to meet Sam during his break, or walk home with him. And she wasn't going to bring up the subject in front of Nancy. That was all the waitress would need to start a string of gossip. No, she would wait until the next morning to talk to Sam.

And when Megan saw him come out of the cabin and start for his car, she hurried outside to catch him. "About the fireworks," she said, meeting him halfway between the cabin and the house, "I wish you hadn't said anything to Josh until you'd talked to me. I really don't see how we can go with you."

"Why not?" Sam stopped and looked down at her. "Neither one of us has to work tonight."

"But I have a lot of housework I need to catch up on."

"On the Fourth of July? On a national holiday?" His eyebrows rose in question. "Come on, Meg, even a woman with responsibilities needs a break once in a while. Josh was telling me about the fireworks and festivities, and it sounded like fun."

He stepped toward her and Megan caught a whiff of his after-shave. It seemed so familiar... as did the blue of his eyes...the sharp lines of his features...the warmth of his smile. Immediately her pulse took off, and her heart seemed to leap into her throat. *Hormones.* How could she possibly spend an entire evening with this man? He made her feel like a love-starved teenager. It was ridiculous.

Megan cleared her throat and tried to be sensible. "Perhaps Josh and I could meet you there."

Sam shook his head. "No, Josh said you don't like to drive at night. That's why I offered."

Darn Josh and his ten-year-old mouth; it looked as if she was going to have to say yes. "Well..." Megan began, hoping an excuse—any excuse—would pop into her head and save her. None did. "You promise no discussions about the guitar?"

"I cross my heart." And Sam did, his fingers brushing over the front of the blue T-shirt he was wearing. "This will be a night to simply enjoy the fireworks. What time should I pick you up?"

She shook her head in disbelief. She had actually said yes!

"Megan, I know you're not wild about having me around, and you think I'm out to corrupt your son. But really I'm not the bad guy. Josh seems so excited about seeing these fireworks, it would be a shame to disappoint him."

"Nine," she said quickly, knowing Sam was right. "You could pick us up at nine."

He grinned. "Too late. I promised Josh I'd buy him a hamburger for dinner. And I also understand there are some activities besides the fireworks...contests Josh said we shouldn't miss. Six all right?"

"Six?" It seemed that Josh and Sam had the entire evening planned. Once again she felt manipulated.

"HEY, LOOK, AN AIRPLANE just took off from the airport." As they neared the outskirts of Grand Rapids, Josh twisted in his seat and pressed his face against the hatchback window to get a better view of the plane overhead.

At the thought of the hand prints Sam was going to have to wash off the car's windows, Megan groaned. She'd told him they should take her car, that he didn't know what he was asking for, putting a ten-year-old in a Porsche. But Sam had insisted. To her relief, Josh was actually behaving quite well, his attention and questions primarily focused on the car's controls and how fast it could go.

She'd listened but said little during the drive. Gazing out the side window, she'd pretended she was watching the rolling hills, scattered woods and verdant fields they were passing. Nevertheless, Megan was always aware of Sam's presence.

He'd dressed casually in a light brown cotton shirt and tan jeans and seemed to be enjoying himself. His dark glasses hid his eyes, but his face was animated and a smile curved his lips. He glanced her way. "Where's a good place to get a hamburger?"

"Burger King," cried Josh from the small back seat.

"If you take Twenty-eighth Street, you'll find your choice of fast-food places," Megan answered.

Sam nodded and, when he reached Twenty-eighth, turned at the signal.

"Over there," Josh said, pointing at a Burger King.

Sam pulled into the parking area, and Megan slid out of the car before he could come around and open her door. After all, they weren't on a date. Seeing the fireworks was for Josh's benefit, not hers. She was just along for the ride.

She'd convinced herself that she could control her responses to Sam, that she wasn't going to let him get to her, but once they were in the restaurant, Megan began to wonder. As Sam leaned close and asked softly what she wanted, his warm breath blew into her ear like a torch and heated her blood. Where was it she'd heard "Blow in my ear and I'll follow you anywhere"? "Ahh . . . I'll have a salad," she stammered, feeling her skin grow uncommonly hot.

This wouldn't do. She had to get hold of herself. As soon as the server handed her a plate, Megan headed for the salad bar.

Josh and Sam took their hamburgers, onion rings and drinks to a nearby table, while Megan moved slowly around the salad bar, piling a bit from every topping available on a bed of lettuce. She hoped the time it would take her to put together a salad would give her a chance to regain her composure.

Sam watched her, a small smile touching his lips. He knew his nearness bothered her and that she was fighting her sensual response. Personally he hoped she lost the battle. He liked her. He wasn't exactly sure why, but he did.

It wasn't that she was extraordinarily beautiful. In fact, in his thirty-four years he'd met many women far more beautiful. And far more receptive. In a way, he supposed, her opposition to him, her disdain of musicians, was a turn-on. At least it was different from wondering if a woman was interested in him or in his reputation.

Megan's plate was now a mountain of vegetation, and Sam was grinning broadly. Soon she would have to give up and join them. Josh was busy eating his hamburger and Sam was glad. It gave him a little more time to study Megan without distraction.

Her white peasant blouse, with its delicately embroidered red and blue flowers across the yoke, had a patriotic look about it. He supposed that was why she'd worn it, and not because it showed off her smooth shoulders or the tempting fullness of her breasts. He wondered what she would say if she knew how much he wanted to touch those breasts. She'd probably tell him to go jump in the lake.

And a tightening in his loins suggested that might not be a bad idea.

The fact that the red cotton skirt that went with her blouse showed off a gorgeous set of legs and nicely rounded hips didn't help cool his libido. He quickly looked away; he had to get his thoughts under control. "How's the food?" he asked Josh.

As Megan approached the table, she noticed Josh was laughing and talking with Sam. The rapport Sam had with her son amazed her. In the past Josh had always acted standoffish with the men she dated. On occasion he'd even been rude. But with Sam, it was as if the two of them had known each other for years.

"Wow, Mom, are you going to eat all that?" Josh exclaimed, watching her slide into the booth beside him.

"It looked good." She kept her eyes lowered so she didn't have to look at Sam.

She ate while Josh began to describe some fireworks her father had brought back from Tennessee three years before. "We weren't supposed to have them," Josh admitted. "They're against the law here. But Grampa said if we were real careful it would be all right. Then he lit one in a bottle and the bottle exploded. After that Mom wouldn't let Grampa play with them anymore."

Sam laughed and Megan glanced up, frowning. She wondered if he saw her curtailment of fireworks as more proof that she was an overprotective mother. No doubt.

Instead Sam's eyes held a glow of warmth and approval. "Sometimes mothers have to remind grandpas to be careful around children."

Megan appreciated his support, but that wasn't what held her gaze. Without words Sam was speaking to her with his iridescent blue eyes, telling her he approved of far more than just her motherly instincts. And Megan couldn't look away. She felt spellbound, totally captivated by a special chemistry that made the moment exciting. It was Josh who finally broke the spell. "Can I have your tomato, Mom?"

Shaking her head to clear the cobwebs from her brain, Megan gave the cherry tomato on her plate to Josh. She was surprised at herself, sitting here gawking at a man.

Sam watched the food exchange, then shifted his gaze to look out the window. He'd seen Megan shake her head and noted the wariness that crept into her expression. *Slow and easy*, he told himself. He didn't want to frighten her. Keeping his eyes on the heavy traffic passing the restaurant, he picked the first topic that came to mind. "Your dad said you were born and raised in Grand Rapids."

"Yes."

"You'll have to give me a tour of the city. Since moving back to the States, I've been enjoying learning about new areas."

Her curiosity was piqued. "Where did you live before?"

"London . . . Paris . . . Rome." Sam looked at Megan. "I was born in Los Angeles, but after my father died my mother and I moved to England. I hadn't been back to the States until four years ago."

A world traveler. That explained his accent. And he'd said he led a stable life. Megan smiled. Not by her standards.

Sam shifted his weight in his seat and his leg brushed against hers, soft denim caressing her bare skin. Electrically charged messages raced up her thigh, and she felt an immediate tightening between her legs that shook her. So much for control. "I'm finished," she said, quickly getting to her feet to dump her still-filled plate.

"Me too," chimed in Josh. "Let's go see the fireworks."

She gave Sam directions to the downtown area and gazed out the window as he maneuvered the Porsche through traffic. She was tense and couldn't seem to relax. Her strong physical reactions every time she was near Sam bothered her. She had to do something about it. But what?

"I doubt if we'll find a parking place anywhere close to the river," Megan said, seeing a traffic jam ahead. "Turn off here, and we can get there the back way."

Sam followed her directions, maneuvering the Porsche with finesse. Determined to keep it casual, she decided to give him that tour of the city he wanted. "I went to school there," she said, as they passed the Kendall School of Design, "and spent a lot of hours there." Her hand motioned across the street, toward the art museum. "Turn here—I want to show you something."

She directed him past Calder Plaza, with its enormous bright orange stabile set in the center, the arching metal rising from the cement. "Grand Rapids is best known for its furniture industry, but when the city planners decided to redevelop the downtown area, they chose a contemporary look and commissioned *La Grand Vitesse*. Alexander Calder finished it in 1959. *Vitesse* means rapids. If you're interested, the rapids on the Grand River aren't far from here, and there's also a very good furniture museum nearby."

"Mom, I want to see the fireworks," Josh cried from the back seat.

"I meant some other time," she explained to her son. "Besides, the museum wouldn't be open today. It's a holiday."

"From all cares and worries." Sam smiled at her.

Megan was amazed when he found a parking place close to the Amway Grand Plaza Hotel. She was never that lucky. Impatient as he was, though, it wasn't close enough for Josh. He scrambled out of the back seat as soon as Sam opened the door and was restlessly dancing from one foot to the other while Sam pulled out a large plaid blanket and locked the car.

They joined the crowd walking down the hill and past the elegant hotel with its multistoried glass exterior. People were already lining the bridge that spanned the Grand River, waiting to see the evening festivities.

Megan pointed out the Gerald R. Ford Museum, a triangular-shaped, modernistic building, and Sam commented, "I was in Paris the day President Nixon resigned and Ford took over. The Parisians loved the scandal." He grabbed Josh's hand to keep the boy from being swept away by the crowd.

The celebration was in full swing, the banks of the Grand River packed with people. For a little while Josh wanted to watch a balloon race, then, too excited to stand still, he pulled them on past the grandstand. There a jazz band was taking down its equipment and the Grand Rapids' symphonic band was waiting to set up for its eight-thirty concert. There were food booths all around, and Josh begged for an ice cream. Sam willingly gave him a dollar, and after her son ran off to the nearest vendor, Megan found herself alone with Sam.

"I think he's enjoying himself." He watched Josh rise up on his toes so the woman behind the counter could easily see him. "I missed out on a lot of this when I was a boy."

"Didn't your parents ever take you to fairs or . . . ?" She wasn't sure what they had in Europe.

Casually Sam reached up to brush a lock of her hair back into place. "From as early as I can remember, my father's health was always too poor for this type of activity. As for my mother, her idea of fun was, and still is, dressing up for an afternoon tea. No, I never got to go to fairs or watch fireworks."

"You said your father died. How old were you?"

"Twelve."

She sighed. "I was fifteen when my mother died. Sometimes I still miss her."

His fingertips moved from her hair to her face, his gaze warm and tender. "You seem very close to your father."

"I am. Now." The touch of his hand was so light that it was like a feather grazing her temple. She stared at his mouth and felt the magnetism. His lips were inviting... just waiting to be tasted, to be— "Want a lick?" Josh asked, tugging on her arm.

"No . . . no, thank you," she stammered, dragging her eyes away from Sam's mouth to look down at her son.

Composing herself as best she could, Megan made a show of glancing around, looking for a place to spread the blanket Sam had brought. She picked out a spot not too far from the bandstand and tried to pretend everything was normal.

But that was easier said than done. The man brought all her senses into heightened awareness. His mere presence was like an aphrodisiac to her. Especially sitting so close on the small blanket. It was inevitable that Sam's arm would brush up against hers, and that his leg would touch her thigh whenever he shifted positions. Inevitable and highly exciting.

When the symphonic band began to play, Josh was immediately and totally entranced by the musicians. Using two sticks he found lying on the grass, he imitated the drummer, rapping on everything available, from empty Styrofoam cups to the side of Megan's purse. Tensely she watched him, expecting Sam to say something. To her relief, he didn't.

With darkness came the fireworks. As the band played Tchaikovsky's "1812 Overture," a multitude of explosions lit the sky, colorful lights reflecting off the water like a myriad of sparkling jewels. Josh laughed with delight and Sam reached over and took Megan's hand. For an instant she froze, uncertain what to do or say, then slowly she began to relax, the warmth of his fingers feeling good and comfortable. She looked his way and he leaned close, his lips lightly capturing hers in a sweet, caring kiss.

Taken by surprise, Megan could only stare—her eyes wide, her mouth partially open. Sam smiled and gave her fingers a squeeze, then looked up to watch the display in the sky.

The kiss had been fleeting; the aftereffect was long lasting. Above and around her there was noise and confusion, but it was nothing compared to the internal confusion she was experiencing. Over and over she asked herself why that simple kiss had felt so good. How one man could be so different from all the others. And why it had to be this man.

She still didn't have any answers to her questions when the fireworks were over. Silently she walked beside Sam as they worked their way back to his car. He casually slipped his arm around her shoulders, but his attention was focused on Josh. The boy's questions were never ending. She was glad. She wasn't ready to face her feelings.

"Do you know 'Rusty Old Rover?'" Sam asked, as he pulled the Porsche into a long line of traffic.

"No," Josh said with a yawn, wadding up the blanket to form a pillow.

"'They call me Rusty Old Rover,'" Sam began, and for the remainder of the trip home he taught both Megan and Josh the words to the humorous old ballad. They drove into the yard laughing.

"Thank you," Megan said, stopping by the back door to face him.

He captured her hand and held it in his, his long fingers wrapping around her small palm. "My pleasure."

He wanted to say more, but didn't dare. He wanted to spend more time with her, time without Josh around, but the wariness he read in her eyes told him not to ask. "Good night," he murmured, and gave her hand a little squeeze. Then he let it go. "Don't let the bedbugs bite," he admonished Josh, ruffling the boy's mop of dark hair.

"Mosquitoes already did." Sleepy-eyed Josh showed Sam the welt on his small arm, then started for the door.

"Good night and thanks again," Megan said softly and followed her son into the house. Sam turned and walked toward the cabin.

It didn't take Megan long to get Josh into bed. He was nearly asleep before his head hit the pillow. She wished she felt as tired. Sleep would be a blessing. Instead she was wide awake and restless.

For a while she puttered around the house, picking up Josh's clothes, straightening the pillows on the couch and rinsing out a few glasses. The house seemed unusually hot and stifling, and she stepped to the back door to look out. She noticed the guest cabin was dark, and she was certain Sam was already asleep. Quietly she slipped outside and walked down to the dock.

A gentle breeze cooled her face and body, the rhythmic lapping of the water along the shoreline making a pleasing sound. Stretching, she took in a deep, refreshing breath. All around her was an orchestra of sound: the twang of the frogs, the hum of insects. A fish out in the middle of the lake jumped, splashing against the water, then a night bird called. Everything was so peaceful.

"Beautiful, isn't it?"

"Ohh!" she gasped, turning to face Sam. Taken by surprise, she laughed self-consciously. "I thought you were asleep."

"I was sitting in the dark, relaxing, and I saw you. Mind a little company?"

What could she say? She'd come out here to think the man out of her system. Talking to him wasn't going to accomplish that goal. Yet she was glad to see him. Torn between wanting to be with him and knowing she was only asking for trouble, Megan wavered in her decision. "I probably should go back inside, before the mosquitoes get me."

He caught her hand before she could leave. "I enjoyed being with you tonight."

Megan tensed, but didn't pull her fingers away. "Josh really likes you."

"And what about you?" His voice was low and seductive.

There was no easy answer to that question. She didn't want to like him. To like him was to invite problems. Yet, in spite of herself, she did. "You're all right," she hedged.

He laughed. "All right?"

"Well, I mean . . ."

"For a musician," he finished for her. His laughter died, but he continued to hold her hand.

It seemed so right, standing beneath the silvery glow of the moon, the sky alive with sparkling stars. Right, and very exhilarating. He smiled down at her, and a warm glow spread through her. She could read so much in his eyes, and what they were telling her was that he liked her, that he wanted to touch her and hold her. And what was worse, she knew her eyes were relaying the same overwhelming desire for him.

"Megan," he said softly, his voice thick with emotion.

Trembling ever so slightly, she continued to stare at his face. She knew he wanted to kiss her, and maybe it was only hormones, but she wanted him to kiss her, too. "Yes?" she whispered.

His arms went around her, drawing her up on her toes. His mouth covered hers, and she arched her body against his, molding her curves to his angles. With a groan of pleasure he began an assault on her senses.

Warm, moving and masterful, his kisses totally captivated her. Her hands went to his sides, to press against the soft cotton of his shirt and find the solid support of his ribs. Her legs felt weak and rubbery, but it didn't matter. He held her close, and she felt secure in his embrace.

Every corner of her mouth was investigated, a foray of little kisses leaving her breathless and excited. He drew her bottom lip into his mouth, sampling its fullness, then let his tongue trace its sensitive inner contour. Automatically she parted her teeth and welcomed his invasion.

Deftly his tongue entered the warmth of her mouth, withdrew, then entered again. Symbolically, he was making love to her, but she wasn't satisfied. Her body was demanding more, and she could feel the hardening of his thigh muscles and knew he wanted more, too. Her fingers tightened their hold, and her palms turned sweaty. She could feel the pounding of her heart, hear her pulse drumming in her ears.

Dizzy and lightheaded, she stared at him when he lifted his head. He smiled at her dazed expression and slid one hand down along her side to find the curve of her breast. His fingers moved over its fullness, his thumb grazing the nipple and bringing it to a firm, hard point. Without a word he was asking permission, and without a word she gave it.

She arched back against the support of his arm, and he pulled her blouse down off her shoulders. For a moment he merely gazed at the full round breasts, the creamy white skin exposed to the cool night air. Then he lowered his head, his curly blond hair brushing against her shoulder, and his mouth covered a taut, rose-colored nipple.

The soft, sucking pressure of his lips sent electrical currents through her body, immediately warming her and igniting even further the fire deep within. She wanted him as she'd wanted no man for years. Frightened, she tried to control the feelings, but couldn't. Nor could she stop her own fingers from lacing through his hair and holding him close.

She hadn't expected to want him—not like this. Not in such a primitive, basic manner. If she didn't stop him soon, she might not be able to stop him at all. "No," she moaned and tried to push him away.

"No?" He straightened up and stared at her, his eyes lambent with passion. Then he nodded. "You're right. We'd better go inside."

Swiftly he pulled her blouse back into place and took her hand. With a step, he started toward the guest cabin, but Megan held back.

"No. I...I can't." Her mind and body were still at odds. Physically she wanted him. Every nerve ending tingled, begged for his touch. But she knew it was wrong. In the morning she would hate herself . . . and him.

First disbelief, then anger transformed his face. "I'm too old to play games, Megan." His eyes were dark with desire and the vein along his temple was pulsing visibly. "Don't say no when you mean yes."

"I mean no," she said, her voice still quavering. "It wouldn't be right."

"What wouldn't be right about it?" His entire body ached for her. "We're two mature adults and..." Sam didn't know how to phrase the rest.

But Megan understood and her eyes narrowed. "And the mother of an illegitimate child certainly shouldn't have any qualms about hopping into bed with a man," she finished for him. Angrily, she pulled her hand free from his. "Let me tell you, Sam Blake, Josh wasn't the result of some casual affair. I'm not a barroom tramp, hot for any and every man who comes along."

"Megan, I've never thought that." He reached for her, but she stepped away.

"In fact, believe it or not, I haven't slept with another man since Rod. And let me tell you, I've been asked."

Her anger made her even more desirable. Hands on her hips, she faced him—her gray eyes stormy, her small chin defiantly jutting forward. He wanted to reach out and touch her short dark hair, cradle her face in his hands and kiss away her doubts. "Maybe I came on too fast," he said, "but believe me, love, I like you. Really I do."

"Ha!" She laughed. "Do you expect me to believe that old line? Don't forget, I traveled with a bunch of musicians for a year. I saw the groupies who followed them and heard the lines the guys gave them. I believe you, all right. I believe you musicians are all alike."

Sam's eyes flashed a warning, but Megan didn't react in time. His hands grabbed her arms and he pulled her to him, so she was pressed against the length of his body and forced to look up. "I won't be lumped into a category," he growled. "I'm a man first, then a musician. So don't go hiding behind a word. I was turned on by you tonight. I thought you felt the same way. Sorry if I misread the signals."

"I—"

"And, while we're on the subject of musicians," he went on, ignoring her attempt to speak. "It's about time you face the fact that your son is a natural. In case you didn't notice it tonight, he was keeping perfect time with that band."

"Leave Josh out of this," Megan cried and tried to pull free of his hold.

"No, I won't. That boy has an ear for music. An innate sense of rhythm. By refusing to let him develop it, you're refusing to recognize a basic part of his nature."

"He's *my* son," she vowed, wriggling harder. "I know what's best for him."

"Sure." Sam snorted in disgust. "Face it, Megan, not having him play is best for you. If he doesn't play the guitar, you won't be reminded of his father, will you?"

He let go of her arms and she stumbled backward, then caught her balance. "That's not true," she said, wishing he could understand her fears.

They stared at each other for a moment, then Sam shook his head. "Good night," he said with finality, and turned to walk off.

"Good night, yourself." Chin held high, shoulders back, Megan marched past him. Maybe it wasn't much of a last word, but it would have to do.

5

IN THE WEEKS that followed, Sam didn't act as if they'd parted on less than friendly terms. He was just as flirtatious as before and continued asking her out. But Megan knew, given the way she felt whenever Sam was close, that it was best to keep their relationship as businesslike as possible. She always had an excuse for not accepting a date.

Josh, on the other hand, grabbed any chance he could to be with Sam. Although Megan knew her son yearned for the attention he was providing, she was afraid Josh was going to be hurt when Sam left. They were all going to be hurt. It was clear that in less than three weeks one curly-haired blonde had had a tremendous effect on their lives.

Business at The Quarter Note was booming. Some nights the tables were filled by eight o'clock, customers actually calling ahead to make reservations. For the first time in months, the ledger showed that they were doing more than just breaking even. It was a relief, but Megan knew the people were only coming because of Sam's fantastic guitar playing, and that scared her.

Every morning she expected to get up and find he'd taken off. It would happen; of that, she was certain. The Quarter Note wasn't big enough or important enough for a man of Sam Blake's talent. One day someone would make him a better offer, promise him stardom. And then he would be gone, and they'd be back in the same position they'd been in before.

It was a problem she was contemplating during the quiet hours of a Monday afternoon, when Sam leisurely wandered into the bar. "Beer?" she asked, after he'd settled himself on a bar stool.

"Sounds good." He looked across the room, where her father was standing on top of a table, working on a ceiling light. "What's the problem, Herb?"

"I'm not sure. It just went out a while ago. I thought it was the bulb, but changing it didn't help. I wish I'd taught electric shop instead of math." The older man glanced over his shoulder at Sam. "Know anything about wiring?"

"Not a thing," Sam admitted. "Maybe that's why I've always stayed away from the electric guitar."

Megan set a frosty glass of beer in front of him. "Hey, I understand you're taking Josh fishing tomorrow morning."

"Josh is taking me," Sam corrected. "He's promised I'll have the best time of my life. Want to come along?"

"At five-thirty in the morning?" Her eyebrows rose as she shook her head. "You've got to be kidding. In fact, how are you going to manage it, after playing tonight?"

"I figure once I get a line in the water, I can just lean back, close my eyes and snooze."

"Oh, is he in for a surprise," Megan's father called from the tabletop.

"What kind of a surprise?" asked Sam, looking at Megan for the answer.

She laughed knowingly. "My son isn't exactly proficient when it comes to casting. You'd better plan on opening those eyes a few times to untangle his line. Still sure you want to go?"

He shrugged his shoulders. "Why not? I can always sleep when we get back. Besides, I can't back out now. I promised Josh I would go fishing with him, and a promise is a promise."

Megan looked at Sam with admiration. In her lifetime, she'd met few men who would get up at dawn, after working most of the night, to take a boy they hardly knew out fishing. "Thank you, I appreciate what you're doing," she said honestly.

Sam said nothing for a moment, taking time for a satisfying swallow of his beer, but his gaze never left her face and there was a smile on his lips when he set his glass down. "Then how about showing your appreciation by having dinner with me tomorrow night?"

"Ah, and here I thought you were taking Josh fishing out of the goodness of your heart. Now I discover you have an ulterior motive. Tsk, tsk." She knew Sam was aware that Sundays and Tuesdays were her nights off, and that she couldn't use work as an excuse, but she wasn't worried. "I'd go, of course—to pay my debt—but alas, you have to work tomorrow night."

His blue eyes twinkled with merriment. "As it happens, last night your dad told me I've been working too many nights and that I have to take tomorrow night off. Looks like I finally get that date with you."

"Dad," Megan gasped and turned her head to stare at her father, "did you give Sam tomorrow night off?"

"Yeah—" He twisted another light bulb into the socket. "He's been working too many hours. We've got to set up a better schedule for him." Stepping off the table, Herb went to turn on the switch.

"Any other excuses you can think of?" Sam asked quietly.

"I don't need excuses." Her eyes locked with his. If he wanted a date, he'd have a date. Dinner certainly would be safe enough. And even if he kissed her good-night, she now knew what to expect. This time she would control her emotions. "What time?"

"Six o'clock?"

"Sounds good. Dad can watch Josh and I won't have to get a baby-sitter. Where are we going? Burger King?"

"No—" he grinned "—I think we'll make it a little fancier than that. Wear something nice." With an easy motion he slid from the bar stool and stood. "Time to see if my suit's clean. See you later, my love."

"I'm not your love," Megan countered.

"Sure about that?" He winked at her and called goodbye to her father. Then, as casually as he'd come in, Sam Blake strolled out.

THE NEXT MORNING, while Sam and Josh were fishing, Megan went through her wardrobe. Her dressy attire was definitely limited. It had been over a year since she'd bought anything new. She laid out a plaid velveteen blazer, tuxedo bow blouse and black flannel skirt. The outfit had looked great three years before at the designers' conference she'd attended in Chicago. Now it looked too businesslike and wintery. Then there was a white, long-sleeved, full-length jersey. She felt elegant whenever she wore it, but it would also be too warm for the temperatures they'd been having. The only other choice she had was a red satin cocktail dress. It was, however, very sexy.

Held up by two skinny spaghetti straps, the bodice not only clearly delineated her full bustline, but also revealed a definite cleavage. Even its red coloring and short skirt seemed provocative. But it would have to do. She had neither the money to buy anything new, nor the time to go shopping.

"Wow!" Josh cried, when she came out that evening, dressed and ready. "You look great, Mom. Doesn't she, Grampa?"

"Beautiful." As he looked up from the easy chair in front of the television, her father's gray eyes mirrored his appreciation. "You know, the older you get, honey, the more you remind me of your mother."

"Really?" Megan leaned over and kissed his cheek. "That's the nicest compliment you could have given me."

"Was Gramma really pretty?" asked Josh.

"Pretty enough to be a movie star, I always said," Herb answered.

"You could be a movie star," Josh decided, giving his mother a scrutinizing look.

A knock at the back door brought Josh to his feet. Scurrying past Megan, he returned leading Sam. Josh was beaming with pride. "See, I told you she looked pretty."

"Very pretty indeed." Sam's gaze traveled over her appreciatively.

Megan herself was busy staring. When Sam played at The Quarter Note, he always wore black, but tonight his black jacket, tailored slacks and tie were a cut above his normal attire. Every line of his suit emphasized the clean masculine lines of his lean body; every stitch spoke of quality. His white shirt looked new, and a red pocket square added just the touch of color he needed. Even his unruly curls seemed orderly.

"Ready?" he asked, his eyes on her face.

"Ready," she answered, magnetically drawn toward him. Forgotten was her vow to remain impassive. "'Night, Dad, Josh," she murmured automatically, as Sam took her arm and guided her toward the door.

Herb McGuire smiled as the screen door slammed behind them and began to hum.

"Whatcha singin'?" asked Josh, going to the window to watch his mother and Sam walk to the car.

"'Some Enchanted Evening,'" answered his grandfather. "They gone yet?"

IN SAM'S CAR Megan found it difficult to shake off the feeling that this was going to be more than a simple dinner date. The redolence of his after-shave and her perfume surrounded them. Soft, romantic music played on the car's stereo. Even the purr of the engine, once Sam guided the Porsche onto the main road to Grand Rapids, added to the romantic atmosphere. In an attempt to break the mood, Megan brought up a topic she knew would be less than endearing to Sam. "I heard you had a few problems this morning."

"Problems," he repeated, giving her a quick, sidelong glance. "That's an understatement. What did Josh tell you?"

"Something about you knocking the can of worms into the lake." She turned slightly in her seat to watch his expression.

Eyes on the road, he nodded, neither a smile nor a frown indicating his mood. "Guilty as charged. Anything else?"

"He said he got his favorite lure caught in a tree." That had been Josh's excuse for no fish, after five hours of fishing.

"Did he happen to mention how long it was in that tree or how he got it back?"

"Nooo." Megan grinned. She was beginning to get the picture. "How long?"

"Two hours." Sam shook his head as he remembered. "He doesn't know how close I came to cutting that line and telling him to forget it. More than once I threatened to, but I'm a sucker for kids with big blue eyes and stories about 'good luck' lures. Not that I could see how any lure that was stuck in a tree could be good luck."

"Two hours?" repeated Megan incredulously. "It took you two hours? What did you do?"

"Everything I could think of. I tried snapping it out, wiggling it out and pulling it out, but I only succeeded in imbedding the hook deeper into the bark. Then I tried standing in the boat, to toss the pole over the branch and get a different angle. But when I stood up—"

"The boat capsized?" she gasped. How could he have been so foolish?

"No, the boat didn't go over, but I did. Do you know how humbling it is to be rescued by a ten-year-old?"

Megan couldn't help but smile. Knowing Josh, she was sure he would have thoroughly enjoyed being the rescuer. "So how did you finally get the lure out of the tree?"

"I climbed it. I couldn't see any other way to get the danged thing."

"You climbed a tree to get Josh's lure?" To Megan that was bravery above and beyond the call of duty. Not even Josh's pleading would have enticed her into a tree.

"At least I didn't fall out." He chuckled. "I think if I had, Josh would have taken the boat and left me there. Nevertheless, I still goofed. When I got back into the boat and reeled up his line, I forgot to keep it taut and ended up with a tangled mess. Your son said I have a lot to learn about fishing."

Megan couldn't keep a straight face. The vision of Josh lecturing Sam was too much, and her laughter filled the small space of the car.

Sam let his eyes leave the road for a second to look at her. She was beautiful when she laughed, her face radiant, her eyes sparkling. Rather than being insulted, he was glad his tale of woe had amused her. Somehow it made his morning's frustrations all worthwhile. And time gave the situation perspective. Now even he could see the humor, and his deeper chuckles joined hers, until they were both laughing freely.

At last she managed to suppress her amusement and, wiping the tears from her eyes, tried to sound sympathetic. "Sam, I'm sorry you went through such an ordeal. However, I did warn you."

"So you did. And I learned. That lucky lure of his went back into the tackle box and after that I told him that whenever he snagged a hook, if we couldn't get it off in five minutes, the line was going to be cut."

"And?"

"I snagged a purple worm in a bush, and we ended up cutting the line. I think we'd have done a lot better if Shady Lake was stocked with flying fish. I swear our lines were out of the water more than they were in. It's no wonder we didn't catch anything but five undersize bass and a bunch of puny perch, all of which Josh insisted we throw back."

Megan couldn't help but feel sorry for him. "I don't think you got much sleep, either. I heard you playing the guitar after you got back home." He'd played long into the afternoon. If he'd taken a nap, it had been a short one.

"Playing the guitar relaxes me."

"And fishing doesn't?" She laughed again.

"Maybe it would if I knew what I was doing. It's another thing I never got to do as a boy. Josh is right—when it comes to fishing, I have a lot to learn."

His confession touched her, and she sympathized with him for all he'd gone through that morning. Yet, at the same time, his lack of fishing skills gave her pleasure. She was glad Sam wasn't an expert at everything he did, and that her son had been a little disillusioned. The camaraderie between Josh and Sam disturbed her. Sitting back in her seat, she tried to analyze her jealousy.

For ten years the only man she'd shared Josh with was her father. Suddenly Sam had stepped into the picture. In little more than three weeks he'd become friend and confidant to her son, and up until their fishing fiasco, it had seemed Sam could do no wrong. Even now Megan doubted if Josh would hold a grudge. Sam was his hero.

A musician. She sighed softly at the irony. Josh hadn't chosen to idolize the banker she'd dated. Or the engineer. He'd chosen a musician.

Megan ignored the fact that she hadn't been overly impressed by the banker or the engineer, either. "Perhaps it would be better if you didn't spend so much time with Josh," she suggested, concerned that her son would be hurt when Sam finally left.

Her comment took Sam by surprise, and the amusement was gone from his eyes when he glanced her way. "What's the matter—afraid I'll corrupt your son with a fishing pole as well as with a guitar?

"No, but . . ."

"But what?"

"I don't want my son hurt."

"And you're afraid I'll hurt him." Sam shook his head in dismay. "My love, I'd never do anything to hurt that boy."

"Maybe not intentionally, but when you leave . . ."

Sam knew there was more she wanted to say. "I think you'd better tell me about Josh's father."

As she was taken off guard, her eyes widened. "About Rod?"

"That was his name?"

"Yes, Rod . . . Rod Parrish."

"And he played the guitar?"

Megan leaned back against the seat and sighed. Why not tell him? Maybe if Sam understood, he would drop the subject. "Yes, Rod was a guitar player and a singer." She glanced at Sam. "Rod had his own group, The Hot Rods, but his dream was to be a big-name star in his own right and have a hit on the charts."

"Did he ever make it?"

"Yes, but not while he was alive. A month before Josh was born, Rod was killed in a car accident. Two months later an album Rod had recorded went gold, then platinum. He *was* good. It was just that he was so damned obsessed with the idea of making it . . . of being a star."

Sam reached over and touched her arm. "Meg, just because Josh's father wanted fame doesn't mean that Josh will."

"But can you guarantee that?" she demanded, facing him, wishing he could. She didn't like playing the bad guy, continually telling Josh he couldn't have a guitar. But she was so afraid. "No, of course you can't," she whispered and let her gaze drop to the long fingers resting on her arms.

"All right then, let's take another approach," Sam insisted, his hand returning to the steering wheel. "Let's say you're right, that Josh is just like his father. Do you really think keeping him away from music is going to make any difference? That not letting him play the guitar will stop him from becoming a musician?"

"I don't know," she said softly, hating to hear Sam ask the same question she often asked herself.

"Well, I do and I can tell you from experience, keeping Josh away from playing an instrument—any instrument—is only going to intensify his desire. He's still a child, but in just a few years he's going to be a teenager, asserting his independence. Don't alienate him, Megan. Talk to him, tell him your fears. Let him know what happened to his father, and why you don't want it happening to him."

"What do I say?" she cried. "I've already told him how hard it is for most musicians to even make a living, that a musician's chances of being a success are slim at best, and that they're surrounded by people always ready to take advantage of them. How do I explain to a boy of ten that the pursuit of fame can turn a basically honest, loving person into a self-centered monster? That his father would allow nothing to stand in his way, not even his own unborn child."

"He didn't want Josh?" asked Sam, slowing as he pulled off the highway.

"A baby didn't fit into the picture, he told me. When I refused to get an abortion, he took off without me." Now she could say it without feeling any pain. At the time, she'd been devastated.

"How old were you then—eighteen?"

"Seventeen. I turned eighteen just before Josh was born."

"You weren't much more than a child yourself." She'd been seven years older than Josh was now. That stunned him.

"I'm not looking for your sympathy, Sam," she responded quietly. "I just want you to see it's more complicated than sitting down with Josh and telling him I'm afraid for him."

Sam pulled the Porsche up in front of the Amway Grand Plaza Hotel. "More complicated, perhaps, but not impossible." He smiled her way. "Let's continue this discussion over dinner."

The doorman helped her out as Sam turned the car over to the valet. They passed through a revolving door and stepped into the lobby of the posh hotel. "I think we go this way," Sam said, steering her gently to the left.

Megan had never been to the restaurant atop the hotel. Cygnus, named for the swan constellation, was known as one of the nicest dining spots in the Grand Rapids area. It required jacket and tie, and she noticed the uniformed attendant in the lobby gave Sam an approving perusal before leading them to the elevator and punching the button for the twenty-eighth floor.

Staring at the glassed wall in front of her, Megan gulped. It was an outside elevator, and heights made her very uncomfortable. The door closed behind them, the elevator gave a jerk and she took in a breath.

She knew from experience that closing her eyes would only make it worse. Steeling herself, she wasn't even aware that she had reached out and grabbed Sam's hand. A swimming pool on the second floor came into view, then fell below. They were picking up speed. Another floor was passed. Then suddenly walls and rooms disappeared and a panoramic view of the city spread out before them. "Lovely," murmured Sam.

"Oh, God," she gasped, gripping his hand even tighter, her eyes widening with fear. It was as if they were taking off in a plane. She was afraid of flying, too.

"Megan, look at me."

She couldn't move.

"Megan . . ."

He pulled her around so she had to face him. The color had drained from her cheeks, and her pupils were dilated. "Don't be afraid," he ordered softly.

"I'm not afraid," she whispered, staring at the back wall. Perhaps if she concentrated on the wooden panels she'd be able to ignore the dizzying sensation threatening to overwhelm her. "I'm not afraid," she repeated, as much to convince herself as to allay Sam's concern. At the speed they were going, it couldn't take long to get to the top. She wouldn't let herself panic. She just wouldn't.

But when the elevator gave a slight lurch, she gasped and squeezed Sam's fingers even tighter. To her relief, they had reached the twenty-eighth floor. The elevator came to a stop, the doors opened and Sam led her out.

"Well, maybe I was just a little afraid," she confessed, immediately feeling better with four solid walls surrounding her. Giving a small nervous laugh, she freed her hand from his.

"Just a little?" He held up his hand, the imprint of her nails still on his skin. Chuckling, he slipped his arm around her shoulders and gave her an affectionate squeeze.

"Dinner for two?" asked the elegantly dressed hostess when they reached her station.

"Blake. I have reservations for seven o'clock."

"I'll call down and see if your table is ready." She picked up the telephone, and Megan glanced around the room.

The ambience was pure elegance. Maroon and gold were repeated in the carpeting, upholstery and cocktail waitresses' uniforms. A huge glass chandelier hung over a curving stairway, and smaller, less ornate lighting fixtures hung above tables set along a glassed wall. Skylights and mirrors gave the lounge an open, airy atmosphere. Even then piano bar had a glass top.

"It will be just a few minutes," the hostess responded, setting down the receiver. "If you'd like to wait in the cocktail lounge, I'll call you as soon as your table's ready."

Sam guided Megan toward a table with a view, but she chose the chair farthest from the window. She was ashamed of her fear, yet unable to quell it. Below them curved the Grand River, beyond and around which lay miniature houses and buildings, streets and cars, covering the landscape as far as the eye could see. Not wanting to think about how high they were, Megan focused her attention on the leggy blonde, dressed in a maroon-and-gold tuxedo-style uniform, approaching their table.

"May I get you a drink?" the woman asked, setting a coaster in front of each of them.

"A Campari and soda," ordered Megan. She could nurse that along. Considering her present state of vertigo, she knew a lot of alcohol was one thing she didn't need in her bloodstream.

Sam asked for a whiskey and water and, after the waitress left, leaned toward the window. "Look down there— you can see where we sat and watched the fireworks." He pointed straight down. "Come over here and you can get a better view."

Megan shifted back in her chair. "I'm fine right here."

He glanced her way. Her face was almost white next to her dark hair, and he realized she was still traumatized. "We can leave, Megan, if you'd like. It doesn't matter to me."

She shook her head. "No. I'm fine. This is something I really should try getting used to." Her smile was forced. "Just don't ask me to look outside."

"Have your ever flown?" He watched her, ready to whisk her out of the restaurant, reservation or not, if the color didn't soon start coming back into her cheeks.

"Once. I was petrified the entire time. It would take a lot to get me on an airplane again. I can't climb trees, either."

"I'll remember that," he said with a grin. "If I ever need to get away from you, I can climb a tree."

"And what are you afraid of, Sam?" she asked, wanting to get her mind on something other than how high they were. "I mean, in case I ever need to get away from you."

"Hmm." He pondered the question. Being used again was his greatest fear, but not one he was about to mention. Better to keep it light. He chuckled, thinking of an answer and knowing there was more truth in it than Megan would probably realize. "What am I afraid of? Why, brunettes with gray eyes, of course. One look and a man's a goner."

Megan laughed. "Oh, yes, I noticed how you quake whenever I'm around."

The sound of her laughter was music to his ears. "I like that," he said, glad to see her beginning to relax. "You should laugh more often."

Immediately Megan sobered. "It's hard to laugh when you're scared. Sam, I know you want to convince me that you're a nice guy... and you probably are. It's just that when I see you, I remember what I went through so long ago, and what might happen if my son decides to emulate you."

"How in heaven's name did you ever get involved with Josh's father?" asked Sam, wishing she never had.

As Megan thought back in time, she let her fingertips outline the pattern of stars on her coaster. "I met Rod at a party. He was in Grand Rapids for a summer rock concert. I was sixteen then, lonely, rebellious and very naive. Rod told me he'd show me the world, and I believed him."

Their drinks arrived. Sam lifted his glass in a salute and tapped it against the side of hers. "Here's to being older and wiser. You ran off with him, I take it?"

"For a year. I was in love. Or at least I thought I was. I was willing to follow Rod anywhere... live in a garret, suffer." Megan shook her head and laughed. "As I said, I was sixteen."

"And when you were seventeen?"

She paused to sip her Campari and soda, and to re-member. "When I was seventeen, I'd had enough of living in the garrets and sharing my food with cockroaches. I'd been to more hick towns than I could remember, eaten in too many greasy spoons, and I'd suffered watching Rod grow more and more determined to make it to the top. He changed so much that year. By the end, he thought only of himself. If he was offered a better contract than the one he had, he'd walk out on a gig. He fired Jeff, his drummer and best friend, because some big-talking talent agent said Jeff didn't have stage appeal. And when Rod was offered a solo spot, he walked out on all the guys. I should have known he would walk out on me, too. My being preg-nant was just an excuse."

"Sounds like a real nice guy." Sam finished his drink and leaned back in his chair. "Not an easy act to follow." Slowly he let his eyes slide over her face. The color was back in her cheeks, and her gray eyes once again held a sparkle. For that he was glad. For the man who had made her so bitter, he had other thoughts. "What do I have to do to prove I'm not like him, Meg?"

"I don't know if you can, Sam," she said honestly, her eyes locked with his. "It's just like my reasons for not wanting Josh to play the guitar. I'm afraid to take a chance. The risk is too great."

"Sometimes people have to take risks or there are no gains."

The intensity of his gaze burned through her, leaving her lips hot and dry. There was no denying the desire she saw in Sam's eyes. He wanted her. And what was worse, she was quite certain making love with him would be a thrill-ing experience. One she would remember for a lifetime. *Take the risk*, her subconscious urged. *Take a chance*. It was tempting, yet she knew that if she had an affair with him, all she would be left with were memories. One day he'd leave . . . just as quickly as he'd come. Megan looked away and took a long, bracing swallow of her drink.

Studying her profile, Sam wished he knew what was going on inside her head. He wondered if he would ever be able to break down her defenses. Get past those memories she had of Josh's father. It was definitely going to be a challenge, but a challenge he was willing to meet.

When the hostess came to say their table was ready, Megan was surprised to discover her glass was empty. She didn't object when Sam offered his arm as they started down the long, curving stairway that would take them to the floor below. And she was glad she had, when the heel of her pump caught on the rug. Her fingers tightened on his arm, and she felt him tense and knew he was ready to catch her if she should start to fall. She regained her balance on her own, but it was a reassuring feeling.

A man to lean on. Someone to give her support when she needed it. It would be nice. But how much could she really trust him? How long would he be by her side? It was difficult to give up old notions. Especially when Rod had taught her so well.

They were taken to a table for two. Maroon napkins in the shape of swans sat on serving plates. A waitress wearing a maroon tuxedo removed the napkins that had been the swans' wings. Laying them on their laps, she asked if they'd like a drink. Megan declined. Slowly her eyes scanned the room.

As with the lounge above, the dining room was walled in glass; the view of the heavens from the skylights—stars twinkling above their heads—was spectacular. And next to their table was a raised marble dance floor, artificial white palms seeming to grow from each corner to form a canopy of snowy white, starched-cloth fronds. A large, maroon semicircle of velvet cut off her view of the musicians' area.

"A bit more elegant than The Quarter Note, I must say," Megan joked, noting the slice of lemon floating beneath the ice in her water goblet.

Much more elegant, she realized when the waitress brought their menus. Megan's eyes widened at the à la carte prices, and she lowered her menu. "Did you see the prices?" she whispered.

"Order what you'd like," Sam said with a smile.

Again she looked at the selections. "Now I know why I've never been here before. In fact, I think we must be paying you too much."

He was having trouble not laughing out loud at her shocked expression. "Look at it this way—with all the times you've refused to go out with me, I've saved enough to pay for this. The medallion of veal with lobster sounds good. Do you want an appetizer?"

Megan glanced at the choices, then again lowered her menu to study his face. "You have me curious, Sam. It's obvious from the car you drive, the clothes you wear...even the way you act...that you have money. Why are you working for us?"

"Because I'm enjoying myself, because you and your dad could use a little help right now, and because, believe it or not, I really do like you."

"Don't say that," Megan groaned.

"I think I'd better tell you about myself," he offered. "Maybe then you'll feel differently."

"No—" she hurried to stop him "—don't tell me anything. I don't want to know about you, I don't want to get to like you, and I don't want you to like me. I've told you from the very beginning, I don't have time to get involved with anyone."

"What if I were a banker?" he asked curtly. "Or a doctor or a lawyer? Would you still feel the same way?"

She truly didn't know the answer to that. "Are you?"

"No."

The hurt she saw in his eyes pained her. "Sam, you've got to understand. It's not *just* that you're a musician. After Rod left me, Dad gave up a lot to help me straighten out my life. He was the one who held my hand when Josh was born, who baby-sat at night, so I could finish high school, and who talked me into going to college. Now is my chance to repay him. I really can't get involved with anyone until The Quarter Note is on its feet."

"Which will be?"

"I don't know. We're doing better, since you arrived, but after you go, I doubt if people will continue driving from Kalamazoo and Grand Rapids to Shady Lake. I imagine we'll be back to where we were before."

"So where's that leave us?"

"Friends?" suggested Megan, and she looked down at the menu. "Sure you still want to spend this much?"

He shrugged his shoulders. "I guess friends is better than being considered a cad. Go ahead, choose whatever sounds good to you." But as she studied the menu he stared at the top of her head. It had been a long time since he'd met a woman who interested him as Megan did.

Megan chose the partridge with truffles, an endive-and-romaine salad, and agreed to share an appetizer of wild mushrooms *en brioche* with Sam. He stuck with the medallion of veal with lobster tail and discussed the wine selection with the waitress. Piesporter was her recommendation, and after taking her first sip, Megan had to agree that the elegant and fragrant white wine did complement the rich flavor of the food.

They had just finished their mushrooms when the mellow sounds of a cornet, accompanied by a piano and drums, filled the air. Slowly the velvet fan next to the dance floor separated at the center and disappeared into a slot in the marble, revealing the three-piece band. "Would you like to dance?" asked Sam.

Other couples were moving from their tables to the dance area. She nodded. It had been years since she'd done a fox-trot, but she did love to dance. Rising to her feet, Megan readily took Sam's hand and walked up the steps to the dance floor.

Her high heels narrowed the difference in their heights, but his head was still above hers. She reached up and tentatively placed her hand on his shoulder, the tight weave of his dinner jacket smooth beneath her palm. His fingers pressed into her waist and he drew her close. When he stepped forward with his left foot, his firm thigh pressed against hers. She quickly stepped back with her right foot and knew that agreeing to dance with Sam had been a mistake. She tried to concentrate on following his lead and not on the turmoil he was arousing within her, but it wasn't easy. She was too conscious of the attraction she felt, of the clean, masculine scent of his body, and of how strong and supple his movements were. He pulled her closer and made a turn, and Megan closed her eyes.

Gazing down at the long, dark lashes touching her cheeks, Sam wondered how long he could keep up this pretext of friendship. From the moment his hand touched the small of her back, he was aware of her vibrant warmth and silky softness. Too aware. Images of her lying naked in his arms, her legs entwined with his, her warmth surrounding him, kept flashing through his mind, and it was all he could do to keep his body relaxed.

"Your hair smells nice . . . like a bouquet of flowers," he murmured, needing something to distract his thoughts.

Megan opened her eyes and glanced up. The look of desire she saw on his face told his thoughts as clearly as if he'd spoken them aloud, and she couldn't stop the quiver of anticipation that traveled down her spine. "Thank you" was all she said.

"You're a good dancer."

"Thank y—" She stopped herself and laughed. "What am I saying? You're the one who's good. I'm just following."

"It takes a good dancer to follow me."

Before Megan could agree or disagree, Sam proceeded to prove his statement. As he executed a complicated series of steps, all amorous thoughts were forced from Megan's mind, her energy channeled into following his lead. Around and around the dance floor they moved, her dancing skills being tested to the hilt. He dipped, he turned, but she continued to move in unison with him.

When the music stopped, she gasped, "Maybe fishing's not your strong point, but dancing certainly is!" She was still clinging to him, her breathing accelerated and her cheeks flushed.

"Only when I have a partner like you." He squeezed her close and touched his lips to hers.

Like molten fire a searing heat flowed from his mouth to hers, igniting her entire body. Her fingers tightened on his shoulder and she automatically rose to her tiptoes, answering his kiss before she realized what she was doing. Then, with a a jerk, Megan pulled back, her eyes wide with surprise. "Friends," she gasped. "We're just friends."

"Friends kiss." He grinned, pulling her back into his arms as the music started again.

Stunned, Megan leaned her head against Sam's shoulder and absently followed his lead as her mind tried to sort through her reaction. Either it was simply hormones, or it was something far more complicated—an emotion she didn't even want to contemplate.

Sensing her inner struggle, Sam said nothing. It was enough, for the moment, to hold her close and enjoy the softness of her body. His movements were automatic, the rhythm of the music his guide. There were no intricate steps to challenge either of them. Now he simply wanted her exactly where she was—in his arms.

When the song ended, Megan stepped back and stared into the blue depths of his eyes. A bond was developing between them. She could sense it. She didn't want to like him, but she did. Turning away, she started back for their table.

He held her chair for her and murmured low, so only she could hear, "You know we're going to be more than friends."

"Sam, don't say that," Megan pleaded, frightened that his words might be true.

"Whatever you wish," he agreed amiably, but there was a satisfied smile on his lips.

Their salads came, and Megan carefully directed the conversation away from personal topics. Movies and books seemed safe enough subjects to discuss, and she discovered Sam had read most of the best-sellers. By comparison, her literary pursuits seemed sorely lacking, and she'd seen none of the movies he had. "You know, I haven't been to a movie rated above PG in years," she mused. "That's what motherhood does to one's movie-going."

"Not even one good bawdy French flick?"

Megan shook her head and laughed. "Not a one."

She enjoyed listening to him talk, his voice as smooth as well-aged whiskey, his faint accent almost lyrical. And when he again asked her to dance, she couldn't think of one good reason to say no. Up the marble steps she went with him, to surrender herself into his arms. Effortlessly they glided across the marble, the magic of the music wrapping itself around them, carrying them along, until the words "friends" and "lovers" became commingled in both of their minds and Megan no longer cared why Sam made her feel so warm and excited.

When they returned to their table, their waitress brought their entrées, but Megan barely noticed what she'd been served. More than once she caught herself staring at Sam, her mind wandering along a pathway of romantic thoughts, her fork poised in midair. And when he looked up and smiled, she knew the hunger she felt had nothing to do with food.

Not once during the evening were they rushed through a course, although waiters and waitresses were ever present to tend to their needs. The food was to be savored, the wine to be drunk, and the music to be danced to. And they did dance—again and again. It wasn't until Sam finished his dinner and Megan ruefully acknowledged that she couldn't finish hers that she realized it was dark outside.

"Sam, what time is it?"

He glanced at his watch. "Ten-thirty."

"Oh, my gosh!" she exclaimed. "We've been here for three and a half hours. I expected to be back before Dad left. Josh is home alone."

Sam signaled for the bill, looked it over quickly and pulled out his wallet. As soon as the waitress had taken his money, they left the dining room and returned to the lounge above. "Sam, do you mind if I call home?" Megan asked, seeing a telephone near the elevators.

"Go right ahead."

Quickly she dialed her number. There was no answer, and she called The Quarter Note. Sam leaned against the wall, listening in, his hand gently caressing her shoulders and neck as she talked to her father. When she hung up the receiver, she sighed in relief and turned to face Sam. "Josh is spending the night with Mrs. Arnosky. When we weren't back by nine-thirty, Dad called her and took Josh over there."

"So there's no rush to get back." His thumb traced the line of her jaw, his eyes on her lips.

She read the desire in his gaze, and her words were husky when she answered. "No, no rush at all."

The elevator doors opened. Sam glanced its way, took in a deep breath and dropped his hand to grasp hers. "Our carriage awaits, madame."

As soon as she stepped inside the elevator, Megan turned her back to the glass wall, hoping the ride down would be better than the ride up. But, at the first shudder of the glassed-in box, she involuntarily gasped.

"What you need is something to take your mind off where you are," murmured Sam, and before she could react, she was securely wrapped in his arms and his mouth was covering hers.

His lips were gentle at first, simply asking for a response. She gave him one, and they became more and more demanding. Megan gripped his jacket for support and rose to her toes. Food had not satisfied the hunger within her. Now her lips moved ravenously over his, searching for and finding their succor. Lights flashed by, cars on the street came closer, buildings grew larger and the elevator groaned. But Megan didn't notice. She was feeding a need that had been increasing from the day Sam walked into The Quarter Note. And when the elevator came to an abrupt halt and the doors slid open, she was still in Sam's arms, feasting on his kisses.

"Hrump." A man waiting for the elevator cleared his throat, and Megan and Sam broke apart.

"Wow!" she gasped, then laughed self-consciously. "No doubt about it, you know how to distract me."

6

"WHERE TO?" Sam asked, as soon as they were in the Porsche. "The night is yours."

"Home." It was too late for a movie, and considering the kiss they'd just shared, Megan was certain going bar hopping wouldn't be a good idea.

In Sam's arms she'd been oblivious to everything but his presence, the feel of his lips on hers and the strength of his embrace. For a few minutes she had forgotten everything but how good it felt to be a woman. That frightened her. Despite her resolve not to get involved, Megan knew Sam was becoming far too important in her life.

As they drove back to Shady Lake, her eyes were drawn to his face. It was such an interesting face. The sharpness of his features showed strength; his clear gaze, perception; and the lines being etched by time into the skin near his mouth spoke of a wry sense of humor. No, he wasn't handsome, but his looks, she decided, were growing on her.

"I'm still waiting for that drawing," he said, glancing over and catching her staring at him.

"What drawing?"

"The one of me with my guitar. Even if I never record these songs I've been learning, I'd like a McGuire portrait."

"A McGuire portrait." She laughed spontaneously. "I like the sound of that. But I've got to warn you that

Gainsborough I'm definitely not. As you've seen, most of the portraits I've done are quite stylized."

"Don't worry about being Gainsborough. I'm not *Blue Boy*, either." He couldn't help but chuckle at the comparison. "It's your abstract style that appeals to me. Your drawings tell more than just what the person looks like. Those sketches in the cabin portray a mood, and that's exactly what I'm looking for."

"All right," she conceded. "Maybe one of these days, if I find time, I could try a few sketches." It would be a challenge to capture the enigmatic qualities that made Sam so different from the other musicians who had come and gone in the past year. She now realized what was wrong with the drawings she'd made of him that first night. They'd showed only the surface of the man, a two-dimensional representation. They hadn't begun to reveal the depth she was discovering he possessed.

"Is Josh also interested in drawing?" Sam asked. A road sign for Shady Lake loomed ahead of them. He took the turn.

"Not the least bit. Oh, he can draw a fairly decent picture, but he'd rather . . . play with his race cars." She had been about to say drum on pots and pans, but had quickly decided against that. No sense giving Sam ammunition for his arguments.

"Your mother was an art teacher, wasn't she?"

"Yes, and a fairly decent artist, in her own right. She did that landscape we have hanging in the living room."

"I thought so. It's nice. Very nice." Personally he'd been more impressed with Megan's work. "Did she encourage you to become an artist?"

Megan's laughter preceded her answer. "Just the opposite. She told me artists are a dime a dozen, that few can make a living from it, and even teaching is a thankless job.

No, she told me to draw for my own pleasure, if I wanted, but to forget it as a vocation."

"Yet you went to art school and became a free-lance illustrator."

It did seem ironic, and more than once she'd questioned why she'd chosen a career in art, especially when she'd first started out and no one was interested in her work. "Actually, I tried to take my mother's advice," Megan confessed. "After I received my high school diploma, I signed up for secretarial school. Josh was just a baby then, Dad was still teaching and I felt I should get a practical job and add to the income.

"I tried to get excited about bookkeeping and typing. Really I did." She looked at Sam, wondering if he could understand. "It was just that drawing seemed to be something I couldn't keep from doing. I'd see an interesting face and want to sketch it; feel sad and need to express my feelings in color and line. When I was supposed to be taking shorthand, my notebook would be filled with doodles. It was Dad who finally convinced me I should give art school a try. Once I did, everything seemed to fall in place."

"And now working at the bar keeps you too busy to draw. That's a shame." He pulled into her drive, shut off the motor and turned in his seat to face her. "Do you miss it?"

"Yes," she sighed. "Drawing and painting relaxes me."

"Like playing the guitar, for me."

And as drumming seems to do for Josh and playing the guitar might, Megan realized. She stared out into the darkness. Maybe Sam was right. Maybe she was burying her head in the sand to think she could keep Josh from being a musician. Or even worse, maybe she was denying Josh an important part of his personality. That possibility bothered Megan.

"Not a cloud in the sky," Sam said, following her gaze.

"It's a beautiful night." She looked back at him and smiled. Her words had included more than the weather. Everything had been perfect—the restaurant, the dancing . . . the kiss in the elevator.

"Megan," he said softly, reaching across the console to gently stroke the side of her face, "close your eyes."

"What?" Her eyes widened.

He chuckled at her obstinacy. "Close your eyes. I'm going to kiss you."

"I don't really think you—" was as much as she got out before he leaned over and silenced her objection.

Although he was persistent, his kiss was gentle, and Megan did close her eyes. Candy, she thought. His kisses were like candy—sweet and tempting. Curiously, she ran the tip of her tongue over his lips. The flavor of an after-dinner mint lingered, enhancing the imagery. His mouth parted invitingly, and she dared to let her tongue enter.

An inner voice warned her to be careful, but she took no heed. Boldly her tongue investigated the unknown, sliding past his teeth to stroke a soft, moist interior. The tightening of his fingers on her arms and the sharp intake of his breath clearly stated that Sam was not impervious to her actions. But she went on playing with his tongue, teasing and titillating.

She knew he wouldn't be able to remain impassive for long, and it didn't surprise her when he pulled her closer. Suddenly it was his tongue that became the marauder, his mouth the aggressor. His lips pillaged and plundered, taking all she offered and asking for more, until she was breathless and weak. And when he lifted his head, Megan could only stare at him, dazed.

"Do you want to go inside?" he asked, his words none too steady. He was cramped by the confines of the car and afraid if he kept kissing her, he was going to go too far. He didn't want to frighten her. Not now.

She hesitated, uncertain. Logic suggested she let him walk her to her door, allow him to kiss her good-night and end the date then and there. But she didn't really want Sam to leave. It had been years since she'd been out with a man who fascinated her as Sam did.

"Just to talk," he promised, seeing her indecision.

She doubted if talking would be all they would do, but it didn't seem to matter. "All right," she agreed.

Sam slid out of the Porsche and paused to light a cigarette before walking around the car to open her door. He frowned at the tremble in his fingers; it wasn't normal for him to get this shaken by a kiss. But then, nothing about his reaction to Megan seemed to be normal. "Your place or mine?" Sam asked, fully expecting her to chose hers.

Megan looked at the cabin and then at her house. "Your place," she decided, not really knowing why, except that in the back of her mind she was thinking her father might show up unexpectedly.

Not that it would matter, she tried to convince herself. After all, they were just going to talk. And even if Sam should kiss her, she was a big girl now. She wasn't going to let the situation get out of hand. Nevertheless, it was the cabin Megan walked toward.

Sam took off his coat and tie and tossed them over the back of a chair. "Wine?" he offered, but she shook her head. She'd had enough alcohol for one night.

The room had taken on the signs of a man's presence. There was dust on the furniture, a pair of dirty socks on the floor near the table and dishes were stacked in the sink. After putting out his cigarette, Sam grabbed the socks and tossed them into the bathroom. Smiling, he strolled toward her. "I didn't expect company or I would have cleaned up a bit."

"It reminds me of Josh's room. I guess boys never get better at housekeeping."

"Girls play house; boys play doctor." He took her wrist and placed a finger on her pulse. "Tell me where it hurts?"

"My feet," she said honestly. "I haven't danced that much in years."

"Your feet?" Sam stepped back and looked down at the thin straps and delicate buckles that held three-inch-high heels to her soles. "Dr. Blake has just the solution. To my office, if you please."

He led her to the couch and Megan sat down. Then he lifted her feet, one by one, to the cushion and removed her high-heeled sandals. "How's this feel?" he asked, beginning to rub his thumb along the rise of her right arch.

"Like heaven." She closed her eyes and leaned back. "Ohh, yes." Every muscle and tendon of her foot responded to his massage, the soreness melting away under the rotation of his fingers.

"And this?" He began to flex her ankle.

"Wonderful." She was relaxing, floating on a cushioned cloud. He took her left foot in his hands and repeated the process, and Megan delighted in being pampered.

Sam watched her, his fingers working the soreness from her feet. Against the background of the beige couch, she looked small and vulnerable, and a surge of protectiveness swept over him. Then anger. "You know, I wish you'd never met that hotshot guitarist."

Megan opened her eyes, surprised by the tight line of Sam's mouth.

"The English have a word for a man like him. Not one I would repeat in front of you." Sam wasn't certain how to classify the emotion roiling within him. Jealousy? Was he jealous of a dead man? Of a man who had touched Megan, made love to her more than a decade before? Never had he been jealous of another man—living or dead. The possibility disturbed him.

"I think every country has a word for someone like Rod. None repeatable." Megan reached out and touched Sam's arm. She could feel the tension in his body and wished she'd never told him about Rod. "Sam, if I hadn't met Rod, I wouldn't have Josh. I regret running off and deserting my father, for being such a fool about a man who didn't deserve it, and for all the problems my immature behavior created, but I'll never be sorry I had Josh. He's like a fresh breath of spring. He's laughter and sunshine. And he makes my life worth living. Maybe Rod didn't want his son, but I'm so glad he gave him to me."

"He also gave you bitterness." Sam's hands continued to work on her legs and feet.

"No, that I chose on my own." She looked up at the ceiling and noticed a tile was cracked. It would have to be replaced. Just as some of her long-held notions would have to be changed. Sam was showing her that. And talking about her mother had clarified her thinking. "You know, you're right, Sam—I haven't been fair to Josh. For years now I've been trying to protect him...keep him from being hurt. But maybe I don't have that right. Maybe it's his decision."

"I suppose it's natural to want to protect your son."

"Still, I don't see how it changes anything. We really can't afford to buy Josh a guitar right now, and he certainly couldn't use yours."

Sam looked to the corner, where his guitar case stood. "No, he can't use the Ramirez. It's too difficult for a child to play."

"And I can't afford to pay you for lessons . . ."

"Megan?" Sam's eyes met hers. "You don't have to pay me. Teaching Josh would be fun. Are you saying you'd let him play the guitar if he had one?"

Megan hesitated before answering. It wasn't easy to change a belief that had lasted ten years. "Yes." Quickly she qualified her answer. "But I still don't want him encouraged. I don't want him having dreams about someday being a big star. If Josh learns to play the guitar, it will be just for his enjoyment. Agreed?"

"Agreed." Sam was tempted to move closer and take her into his arms. And he might have, if she hadn't gone on.

"Still, it's impossible. We can't afford a guitar. Not now."

He smiled. "There are always used guitars available, sometimes at quite reasonable prices. Leave everything to me."

"Sam, we can't afford even a reasonable price." Whatever that might be. There were other bills that had to be paid first.

"Then I'll buy one for him."

"No." Her answer was firm.

"Why?" His fingers stopped their kneading action, and he stared into the dark gray of her eyes.

"Because we owe you enough. Because . . ." She didn't know why.

"If it bothers you to owe me, you can pay me back when you have the money."

"You're doing too much for us."

"And you don't want to feel obligated, right?" He didn't know how to tell her he was getting as much back from her and her family as he was giving. To confess how much she meant to him would certainly frighten her away.

"I don't know. . . ." She looked at the ceiling again, at the wall and, finally, at him. "Oh, Sam." Megan sighed, knowing she had to consider her son's feelings as well as her own. "All right. You buy Josh a guitar and I'll pay you back as soon as I can. And if you're not still here, I'll mail you the money."

"Always trying to get rid of me, aren't you?" He grinned and let his fingers roam up her legs to her knees.

The tightening in her groin was automatic, her intake of breath audible.

"I'm not leaving, my love. Not for a long time." His eyes on her face, Sam slowly brought his hands back down to her ankles. "Your feet feel better?"

"Yes." Her heart was beating wildly, the blood pounding in her ears. His touch had excited her and her body wanted more.

"Good. Since you're so concerned about paybacks, it's your turn."

Her eyebrows arched quizzically. "My turn?"

Sam scooted up next to her hips and turned his back to her. "Since we're playing doctor, it's your turn to treat me. Left shoulder. I think I pulled it when I climbed that tree this morning."

"That's what you get for trying to play Tarzan." Megan chuckled and tentatively rubbed the heel of her palm over his shoulder blade. She felt relieved now that the issue of Josh's playing the guitar had been resolved. Maybe she could find time to do some advertising copy. Westmount Furniture Outlet was always running ads and looking for free-lance illustrators. They didn't pay well, but if Sam really did find a guitar at a reasonable price, it might not take her long to pay him back.

His shirt bunched under her fingers. "I never played doctor as a child, but isn't part of the game to get the patient to undress? Take off your shirt, Mr. Blake." She imitated a lecherous laugh.

"Aha, now the party's getting good." Willingly he unbuttoned his shirt and pulled it from his pants. In a moment the fine silk cloth was in a heap on the floor. "How's that, doc?"

"Better. Now I can see what I'm doing." There were small red scratches all over his arms and shoulders. "Did you get these climbing that tree?" she asked, touching one.

"Yes." He flinched and started to pull away, but her hand on his arm stopped him.

"Sam, you do too much for us. You didn't need to go out fishing with Josh or climb that tree." She began to rub his shoulder. "If you'd fallen out, you could have killed yourself, broken an arm . . . anything."

"But I didn't." He turned his head; the way she was positioned he still couldn't see her face. The feel of her small hands on his back was disconcerting, and he rolled his eyes upward. If she knew what her nearness was doing to him, she'd run like hell out the door. How long he could resist taking her into his arms, he wasn't sure.

"I like Josh," he said, his voice none too steady, "even if he does need a few lessons in casting, which he obviously isn't going to get from me."

Megan could sense the tension building within Sam. She was having her own problems keeping her mind on massaging his shoulder. Touching him, actually feeling his supple strength beneath her fingertips was driving her crazy. She wanted to hold him close, press her cheek against the warmth of his tanned skin and breathe in his unique smell. She longed to kiss away the scratches and bring relief to his sore body. The desire was so strong that her hands began to shake.

Sam felt the tremors and turned so he faced her. "Megan?" Her smoky gray eyes beckoned him to share her fantasy, and he took her into his arms and drew her close, knowing she would offer no objections. "Talking's not enough for either of us, is it?"

"I don't know what's come over me," she confessed, her entire body trembling.

"I think I do." Confidently he claimed her lips.

Her mouth was soft and pliant beneath his, giving as well as receiving. Hip to hip they sat, her arms going around his back in a passionate embrace, his bare chest pressed against the bodice of her dress. Beneath the satiny material her breasts began to swell, yearning for his touch.

But Sam ignored the invitation. He was in no rush. His hands were busy moving over her back, his lips occupied with her face. He was discovering the feathery feel of her incredibly long lashes against his cheek, how she arched toward him when he kissed her ear, and the flowery scent of her neck. Everything about her pleased him, from the glow of her skin to the rich texture of her hair.

And when he did slide the zipper of her dress down and slip the straps from her shoulders, it fell in soft folds to her waist. Sam unsnapped her strapless bra and let it drop to the floor. Half-naked, Megan sighed, snuggling close. It felt so right to be in his arms, to feel his warm flesh touching hers. The hairs on his chest brushed against her breasts and teased her nipples to rigid peaks. "Nice," he murmured, his hands moving from her back to her sides.

"Hmm," she agreed, knowing she'd never felt as cherished as she did at this moment.

"So soft and feminine—" he sat back and held her away from him, so he could look at her "—and beautiful." His eyes traveled over the full, rounded curves of her firm breasts, then returned to her face. "Very beautiful." His smile was loving. "From the moment we first met, I've wanted to hold you in my arms like this, to touch you . . . discover the secrets of your body."

"No more than I've wanted to know yours," she confessed somewhat shyly. She reached out to stroke his chest. His nipples were as hard and erect as hers, and she brushed her fingertips over them.

Sam watched her playful gesture for a moment, then cupping her breasts in his hands, he let his thumbs trace a pattern around each bud before actually rubbing across the peak. The dark brown of his skin contrasted to the milky white and pink of hers, the roughness of his hands to her smoothness.

He kissed her again, wanting to renew contact with her lips. Her mouth met his eagerly. The throbbing pressure in his loins begging to be released, he turned his body to stretch out on the couch, pulling her with him and wedging her between his length and the cushions.

Megan twisted to find a more comfortable position, her hips rubbing against his. Her dress was wrapped around her waist, the hem pulled up and revealing a length of thigh. She could feel the hard line of his arousal, but didn't pull away. It seemed right that they were this close. Everything about the evening had brought them to this moment.

Their kisses were growing longer, their need a persistent ache. Hands moved provocatively over heated flesh, stimulating primitive impulses, and Megan forgot about friendship and caution. It didn't matter that he was a musician and would one day leave. Tonight she wanted to take him into her body and absorb his strength.

"Megan, I don't want to stop," Sam warned, boldly sliding his hand under her slip and panties.

"I don't want you to stop," she admitted, his probing fingers setting her on fire.

Silky curls caressed his palm, a liquid warmth confirming her readiness. His breathing ragged, he could barely speak. "Let's go into the bedroom."

Her emotions were jumbled, a desire to feel Sam within her paramount to all else. He rose to his feet and helped her up, her dress dropping to her ankles as she stood. "Sam?" Megan paused. Her legs were trembling and her breathing was shallow. What was she going to ask him, anyway? If he loved her? Of course he didn't. And she didn't love him; loving him would only bring sorrow. No, what they each felt was physical—that was all. But she did need to exercise some caution. "I'm not protected."

"I'll take care of that." He kissed her and slid his arm around her shoulders.

Megan stepped out of her dress and walked barefoot to his bedroom. Unmade from his afternoon nap, his bed was a jumble of sheets and covers, but it didn't matter to either of them. Sam simply cleared a spot and straightened the pillows, then pulled her down with him onto the cool, inviting sheet.

Heated hands roamed her body, while demanding kisses commanded her lips, followed his hands, then returned to her lips. Her slip was removed, then her panties, and he stroked and kissed the newly exposed area with a fervor that sent her spiraling. Megan gasped. His roving tongue had found its way between her legs. "I...oh, Sam..." The room was spinning, her control tenuous. "I'm going to...I..." Her fingers dug deep into his hair, speech impossible as waves of pleasure began to shake her body.

She was barely aware when Sam stood and removed the rest of his clothes. Only when he stretched his body over hers did it register that she'd been the only one satisfied. And, as he kissed her, greedily taking her lips, she wondered if her own needs had been truly met. His touch still turned her to fire and his kisses still stimulated a desire to surround him. She reached down between them to stroke his sensitive skin, and he groaned in pleasure. Unable to wait any longer, he came to her.

Their bodies blended soft to hard, and her legs wrapped around his. Slowly Sam nurtured her unquenched desire, leading her in an upward flight—a flight that held no fear, only the promise of delight. Higher and higher she soared with him, to an atmosphere where the air was rarified and breathing difficult. Quivering, she clung to his arms, wanting the sensations to go on forever, yet certain she would die if she had to wait another second. And when Sam found his release, he triggered within her a climax that surpassed her first. Totally satisfied, she floated back to reality, content in Sam's embrace.

Lying beside him, Megan felt lethargic, a sense of well-being erasing all concerns. Opening her eyes, she looked at Sam and smiled.

"I knew it would be good between us," he said, the sound of his voice mellow and relaxed.

Good? The word seemed sorely inadequate. Never had she experienced anything so exhilarating . . . so over-whelming . . . so completely satisfying. Lovingly she stroked his cheek, wishing she could voice her feelings, but afraid to let him know how deeply their lovemaking had affected her.

Sam fell asleep beside her, his head nestled against her shoulder, one arm draped possessively across her hip. Megan knew he had to be exhausted after his morning with her son and having had only a few hours sleep. Her own body was demanding rest, but she didn't dare let herself doze off. It was late, and her father would be closing the bar soon. She had to get to her own bed. "Sam?" She nudged him gently. "I've got to go."

He mumbled something unintelligible and moved, his arm sliding off her hip, but he didn't wake up. Megan gazed tenderly at the man who had just given her so much pleasure. Silently she slipped out of his bed.

7

JOSH WAS ECSTATIC when Megan told him he could play the guitar and that Sam was going to find one for him and would give him lessons. By the weekend Josh had his guitar—used, but in good condition, the price more than reasonable, as far as Megan was concerned. A bit of scrimping and saving would pay it off in no time, eliminating the necessity of taking on extra work. As much as she liked drawing, creating furniture ads was not her favorite pastime.

She soon learned that if Josh wasn't with Sam, studying technique, she could usually find him practicing. Even sore fingers didn't diminish her son's enthusiasm, and Megan had to admit the sounds Josh now produced were far more enjoyable to listen to than his usual thumping on furniture.

As for Sam, Megan had expected their night of lovemaking to lessen the attraction she felt for him, but discovered, instead, that knowing him intimately had only increased her interest. Despite her resolve not to, she'd become involved with him. So when her father again mentioned setting up a work schedule for Sam, Megan saw to it that Sam worked those nights she was off. That, combined with Josh's presence during the day, left no opportunities for her to again succumb to Sam's charm. However, living so close, she saw him often.

He'd go swimming when she did, would come outside to practice while she was working in the yard and often stopped by for coffee with her father. And, in spite of his rotten first experience, Sam took Josh fishing again and again, even hiring a local fisherman to give both of them lessons in casting. So when Megan decided the doors and trim around the house couldn't go through another harsh Michigan winter without a fresh coat of white paint, she wasn't really surprised when Sam pitched in and helped.

"Uh-oh, you're getting white hairs." Megan laughed and pointed to his head.

"If so, it must be from frustration," Sam muttered. Cautiously he reached up and touched a sticky mat of curls, then remembered the drip that had rolled from his brush, when he'd stretched to catch a spot above his head.

"So what are you frustrated about?" They'd finished the painting and were cleaning their brushes. She thought it had gone well; the house looked good.

"When do I get to see you again?"

"You're seeing me right now." Their relationship was one topic she didn't want to discuss. Moistening the end of a cloth in paint thinner, Megan hoped to change the subject. "Bend over and let me get that paint out."

He obeyed, but didn't let her off the hook. "You know what I mean. It's been three weeks since we went out to dinner. Three weeks since we—"

"Sam," she interrupted, knowing he was going to mention their lovemaking. "I've been busy. We've all been busy."

It was true. Two weeks before, her father had begun placing advertisements in all the metropolitan and local papers—headlining Sam as The Quarter Note's star entertainer. And it was paying off. Clientele had increased to the point that their ledger was now showing a definite profit, making Megan fear even more than before the day Sam would take off and leave them high and dry. "Sam, how long are you going to stay?" she asked, stepping back, the last of the paint out of his hair.

He straightened his long body and looked her right in the eye. "I don't know for certain. Trust me, Meg—I'll let you know when I feel I have to leave. I won't run out on you."

She knew he was referring to her experience with Rod. "I do trust you more than I did at first."

"But not enough to spend another night with me." Sam's gaze was unrelenting. "Don't you think I know who set up that work schedule?"

"It was the only possible arrangement," Megan lied.

"Sure." His brows rose skeptically. "Since you're afraid to be alone with me, how about letting me take Josh and you to the Ionia Free Fair tomorrow?"

"I'm not afraid to be alone with you," she said, turning away to clean her brush. That she didn't trust herself was closer to the truth.

"If you say so." He didn't sound convinced. "Will you go?"

"How can we?" She worked the paint out of the bristles and gave the brush a good rinsing. "You have to work tomorrow night."

"Not until nine." Sam watched her, but she avoided looking at him. He hadn't been surprised when she'd given him the cold shoulder after their lovemaking. His falling asleep and not even knowing when she left hadn't been the best of moves. But after three weeks he felt he'd made amends, that she couldn't still think it was only her body he was after. And he was inviting Josh along, too. "What do you say? Will you go?"

Megan had no intention of refusing his invitation. She had Sundays off, and a day at the fair sounded like fun. Putting her brush down, she faced Sam and smiled. "You've got yourself a date, mister."

SUNDAY COULDN'T COME fast enough for Josh. "Can I ride the roller coaster?" he begged. "I'm big enough."

"I don't know. You know I don't like you going alone. Maybe Sam will ride with you." Her fear of heights kept her off most of the midway rides, a weakness Josh couldn't understand since for him the higher and scarier the better.

Except for the rides that stayed firmly on the ground, Megan declined to go on any, and it was her father who had to accompany Josh, although even he never rode on the roller coaster or any of the really good rides, according to Josh. "Aw, Mom, you're just a scaredy-cat. What's going to happen to me, anyway? I'm too big to slip out from under the bar and I know enough not to get up while a ride's moving."

"Maybe I am a scaredy-cat," Megan responded, giving Josh an affectionate hug, "but I love you too much to take a chance that something might happen. You can't ride the roller coaster or any of those other thrill rides unless Sam goes with you."

"What if Sam doesn't want to go on any of those rides? What if he just wants to walk around and look at things, like you do?" With a pout, Josh pulled away from her embrace.

But Josh didn't need to worry. Sam willingly agreed to ride the roller coaster, the double Ferris wheel, the swinging pirate ship and all the rides that sent Megan's heart to her throat. Standing firmly on the ground, Megan watched, her ears being numbed by the blaring rock music that emanated from each ride and her body jostled by the crowds. At last, after nearly two hours, Sam took pity on her. "I think your mother's had all she can stand, champ," he said, tousling Josh's hair.

"But all she's been doing is watching." Josh shook his head, unable to understand grown-ups.

"Watching you spend all Sam's money," she admonished. "Those rides cost a fortune, Josh. It's time we do something else."

"Can we eat? I'm starved." Josh grabbed both Megan's hand and Sam's and started for one of the food concession stands.

"After all those ups and downs?" She knew her stomach would have rebelled at the idea.

But ups and downs didn't affect Josh's appetite. Two hot dogs, a large helping of French fries and a Coke later, he was begging for ice cream. "I'll pay for it," said Megan, handing her son a dollar before Sam could reach for his wallet. "You've already spent too much on us." Although admission to the fair was free, the cost of the food, games and rides seemed exorbitant to her.

Sam pushed his paper plate aside, only a few French fries left from his hamburger, and reached for his iced tea. "Coming here was my idea, so stop worrying about money. Now that we've satisfied Josh's desire to scare himself...and me...to death, what would you like to do?"

"I'd like to see the exhibits, if you wouldn't mind." The crafts always fascinated her. "And the animals."

"Exhibits and animals it is." Sam took her hand, and they rose from the table to find Josh.

The Ionia Free Fair was the largest of its kind and for over seventy years had enticed huge crowds to come view its exhibits, to sit in its grandstand and watch pulling events or fine country and western entertainment, to enjoy its enormous midway and to gorge on everything from "elephant ears" to ultrasweet cotton candy. By the time they'd walked through all the display buildings and animal barns, Megan was limping. "I've got to sit down for a while," she said, and headed for a bench inside the 4-H building.

"Hey, Mom, I've got a joke," Josh said, settling himself between Megan and Sam. "What part of your body belongs in a barn?"

"I don't know." Megan unstrapped her right sandal and checked the side of her foot. "What part of my body does belong in a barn?"

"Your legs."

"Legs?" She saw the start of a blister near her little toe and wished she'd worn her more comfortable, if not stylish, work shoes.

Josh frowned when she didn't laugh, then realized his mistake. "I mean your calves."

"Calves?" Megan looked at her son, surprised that his joke actually made sense. Then she laughed. "That's a good one."

"It is, isn't it?" he agreed, beaming.

"Actually, I think he's trying to give you a little bull," interjected Sam. "Do you need a Band-aid for that blister?"

Josh groaned at Sam's pun, but Megan laughed even harder and shook her head. "It'll be all right, as long as we don't do much more walking. Okay now, I've got one for you two," she said, putting her sandal back on. "If you have a brown egg, on a red table, in a green box, where did the egg come from?"

Sam and Josh looked at each other, shook their heads and shrugged their shoulders. "I don't know," Josh answered. "Where did the egg come from?"

"A hen. Boy, you two sure don't know much about farming, do you?" She stood, laughing, delighted that she'd tricked them.

"Fowl joke," Sam complained, his chuckles accompanying hers as they left the building.

"Know why the chicken crossed the road?" Josh picked up, skipping beside them.

"To get to the other side?" both Megan and Sam answered in unison.

"Nope, to lay that egg on the red table."

"Corny," laughed Megan.

"Chicken," giggled Josh.

Sam groaned, "This is getting bad. I think it's time we go get a Coke."

Still laughing, the three of them wove their way through the boisterous, congested midway to the tent that held the free Coca-Cola shows. Sipping Cokes and resting, they listened as a high school vocal group tried to sing over the noise of the public address system and the helicopters that regularly flew above the fair grounds, carrying passengers on paid rides.

"Time to go," Sam stated, when the group finished its stint and a dance studio took over the entertainment.

"Yeah, who wants to watch a bunch of dancers," agreed Josh. "Let's ride the Super-loop again."

Sam looked at Megan and shook his head in dismay. "I think I must be getting old. I'm beat."

Megan was in total agreement and stood to leave. "Josh, no more rides. We have to go. Sam has to work tonight and we don't want him so tired he can't play."

Longingly Josh gazed at the ride area, then sighed and turned to walk with them toward the parking lot.

"Thanks, Sam," he remembered to say, before getting out of the Porsche, back at the house.

"My pleasure," responded Sam and watched the boy run into the house to tell his grandfather what they'd seen and done. Then Sam's eyes returned to Megan's face. "Did you have a good time?"

"Yes," she answered honestly. It seemed the more time she spent with Sam, the more she enjoyed his company.

Sam took her hand as they walked toward her back door. From inside they could hear Josh's high-pitched voice describing ride after ride and Herb McGuire's occasional deep-throated response. At the doorstep Sam stopped, his fingers still entwined with hers, and Megan looked up and knew he wanted to kiss her.

And she wanted to kiss him. It seemed the perfect ending to a perfect day. Tilting her head back, she leaned toward him, and he accepted the invitation, his lips brushing lightly over hers. Then his mouth returned for a deeper, more satisfying kiss.

Hungrily he tasted her lips, wanting to totally possess her but knowing circumstances were against him. "When can we be together, alone?" he whispered huskily, his hands shaking slightly when he rested them on her shoulders.

"I don't know," answered Megan, a burning deep within her suddenly making her wish she hadn't worked so diligently on his schedule.

"These past three weeks have been driving me crazy," he rasped, his grip tightening and his voice pitched so low that neither Josh nor her father could hear. "I want to hold you, be with you."

"I want to be with you," she whispered, wishing they could silently slip into his cabin and steal a few hours—all the while knowing it would be impossible.

"Tomorrow? Is there someone who can take Josh in the morning, while your dad's gone?"

"Not tomorrow." She closed her eyes in frustration. "Josh has a dentist appointment in the morning."

"Megan, I can't take it any longer," Sam groaned. "You've got to change my work schedule. I want a night I can be with you."

"But the ads..." she began, then stopped. The heck with the ads. "I'll work on it tomorrow."

SHE PLANNED ON CHANGING Sam's schedule Monday afternoon, but a lonely, talkative customer took up her time. It wasn't until eight that evening that she had a chance to jot down alternative scheduling possibilities. Sam had Monday and Wednesday nights off. The question was whether to give him Sunday or Tuesday night off, too.

"Whatcha doing?" asked Nancy, coming up to the counter and glancing over Megan's scratch pad.

"Working on a schedule for Sam. He wants more time off." Megan hoped her answer sounded nonchalant. She didn't need the young waitress's suspicions.

"Hmm, the same nights you have off?" Nancy's pencil-thin eyebrow rose.

"Well, we certainly can't give him Fridays or Saturdays off, and he's been drawing quite a crowd on Thursdays. Do you have any suggestions?" There, she would leave it in Nancy's lap.

"I suppose you're right," Nancy agreed. "Hey, the table by the piano wants a Quarter Note Special. Doubles on the crackers."

"I'll get right on it." Megan put her pencil down and headed for the cooler for the cheese and sausage.

Monday nights were so slow that Nancy and Megan usually worked them alone until ten, when her father came on duty. Harry Baldwin, the local sheriff, checked in off and on just to make certain everything was going all right. Megan halfway expected him, so when the door opened, she assumed it was Harry. However, when she looked up she saw a complete stranger heading toward the front bar.

He was wearing a pin-striped business suit, and Megan guessed his age to be around forty, touches of silver highlighting his dark brown hair, horn-rimmed glasses framing his large brown eyes, and a widening midriff indicating he wasn't in the best of physical shape. Nancy was still lounging by the counter, waiting for her order. He walked directly to her and asked a question. Nancy shook her head, he said something else and Nancy laughed and called out, "Megan, come over here, you've got to hear this."

Wiping her hands on her apron, Megan left the plate of cold cuts to see what was so amusing. The man smiled at her and she returned the smile, noting his teeth had been capped. "Calvin Monroe," the gentleman introduced himself, extending his right hand toward Megan. "Just call me Cal. You must be Megan McGuire. Sebastian's told me about you."

"Sebastian?" Confused, Megan's eyebrows rose in question as she shook his hand.

"You probably know him as Sam, but I always call him Sebastian. It certainly wouldn't do for me to say Sam Blake when promoting Sebastian Blake, would it?"

"No, of course not," she agreed, not certain why it would make any difference.

"When I talked to him, he gave me directions on how to find where he's staying." Cal pulled out a piece of paper with a penciled map and laid it on the bar in front of Megan. "I think I found the right place, but no one was there, so I figured the best thing to do was stop by here."

Megan glanced at the map. The directions were clear and concise. There was no way he could have been to the wrong cabin. "Sam's gone into Grand Rapids to see a movie with my dad and son. They won't be back until after nine. His name's really Sebastian?"

Nancy giggled and Megan glowered at her.

"Sebastian Augustino Blake," Cal said proudly. "But surely he told you?"

Both Megan and Nancy shook their heads and Cal looked ill at ease. "Have you ever heard of Andrés Segovia, Julian Bream or John Williams?"

Megan nodded at the first two, Nancy only at the mention of Segovia's name. "Are you saying Sam...Sebastian is...?" Suddenly all the hours Sam spent in his cabin practicing began to make sense to Megan.

"Is one of the best classical guitarists alive today. He's played with the London Philharmonic, in concerts throughout Europe, for royalty, heads of state, prime ministers..." Calvin Monroe gestured dramatically with his hands, his voice rising with each accolade.

"I've never heard of him," said Nancy, shaking her head.

Cal looked crestfallen and sighed. His hand dropped back to the counter. "I'll admit Sebastian's better known in Europe. I keep trying to get him to accept more concerts and guest appearances here, but he refuses to do more than a few a year."

"You're his agent," Megan said, verbalizing her realization.

"Agent and friend, I like to think. Who but a friend would fly all the way from New York to Grand Rapids and back the next morning, just to get an okay on a contract?"

Megan's stomach twisted. From her days with Rod, she knew about contracts. They meant gigs and money. They meant moving on to new places.

Neither she nor her father had thought to have Sam sign a contract. He was free to leave anytime he wanted. And with his agent standing in front of her, Megan was certain Sam would be doing just that—and soon.

Without realizing it, she clenched her fists, her nails digging into her palms. She felt deceived. Deceived and angry. "I suppose you're also going to tell me he has a wife and three kids," she muttered.

"No wife," Cal said, "but there are about twenty kids who miss him."

"Wow, he's been busy," gasped Nancy, her eyes widening.

Cal laughed heartily. "Not that kind of kid. Underprivileged ones. Whenever he's in New York, he volunteers his time at a boys' club and gives guitar lessons."

"How noble of him." Megan's words oozed sarcasm. "And just think, now he's found another underprivileged child to teach."

"Josh is hardly underprivileged," scoffed Nancy.

Cal noted Megan's touchiness and changed the subject. "Think you could fix me one of those?" he asked, pointing to the dish of cold cuts she'd been working on. "And a Scotch and water?"

"Coming right up," Megan said a little too smoothly. Moving back to her work station, she reached for a highball glass.

"I suppose I should have called him and let him know I was coming," Cal went on, making conversation as Megan worked. "But when this deal came through I decided on the spur of the moment to hop a plane. I figured it would be harder for him to say no to me in person than on the telephone." Cal sighed. "Can you believe it, the New York Philharmonic wants him to do a guest performance, and I'm going to have to convince him to take it." He shook his head. "Sometimes I wish the man needed the money. You might have heard of him by now, if he would accept even half the guest appearances he's been offered. Or if he'd cut a record or two. But no—" with a nod he accepted the drink Megan handed him "—Sebastian would rather take six months off and go traipsing around the countryside, writing down old folk songs. And now he's talking about recording them." Again Cal shook his head. "Sebastian Blake playing folk songs?"

"They sound good," Megan said, wondering why she was even defending Sam.

"He's real good," echoed Nancy. "Why, he packs this place every weekend."

Cal looked around The Quarter Note, and Megan could tell from his expression that he wasn't impressed. She was already on the defensive when he spoke. "Sebastian said you needed help."

"We're not a charity case," Megan snapped.

"Oh, no, I didn't mean to imply that," Cal hurried to insist. "From what he's said, I think Sebastian is actually enjoying playing here. And the money you're paying him is going for a good cause. He's donating all his wages to that boys' club."

"A veritable saint," muttered Megan, slapping two packages of crackers on the tray. She handed Nancy her order and reached for a clean plate. As she began working on Cal's order, the image she projected was of an efficient, speedy barkeeper, but inside she was seething.

She could see the headlines already. *"Big-name guitarist aids failing bar"*. Yes, indeed, the man was a saint. *Saint Sebastian*. Megan hacked off a slice of summer sausage. At the moment, the idea of shooting a few arrows into Sam was appealing.

They didn't need his charity. Maybe they had been having problems when he showed up, but they could have solved them. He was slumming, that's what he was doing. Playing the do-gooder. Well, he could just go act the part of the philanthropist with someone else. She'd be damned if she would feel obligated to him. And he could sign that contract his agent had flown so far to give him and get out of their lives. They would do just fine without him.

Or would they? Megan wondered, getting a wedge of Colby cheese from the cooler. In one month Sam's presence had changed the ledger from red to black. He'd become like a son to her father, and like a father to her son. As for her... Setting the plate of food in front of Cal, Megan tried not to think about her feelings. The ache filling her was too confusing.

"I'm not surprised that no one around here has recognized him." Cal reached for a slice of sausage. "He never uses his picture on any album covers or billboards. Just artistic renditions of him playing. But I bet people start recognizing him soon. This year I have a five-city tour lined up for Sebastian: Boston, Philadelphia, Chicago, San Francisco and Houston. He's never played in Texas, but they're really enthusiastic."

Megan busied herself with cleaning her work area while Cal ate and talked. He described the acoustics in the different halls and how Sebastian's concerts were fast becoming sellouts. The more Megan heard, the harder it was to keep the tears from her eyes. He was leaving. Really leaving. She'd known the day would come and now it was here. The stark reality of that fact was tearing her apart.

Finally Cal finished his food and the last of his drink. Standing, he reached for his wallet. "How much do I owe you?"

"It's on the house," she responded tightly. "Sam's done a lot for us. It's the least we can do for his agent."

"Thanks." Cal glanced at his watch. "You said he'd be around after nine? It's nine now. I think I'll go on back and wait for him. Any messages you'd like me to deliver?"

"Tell him he's a man of many surprises," Megan said, sounding far more composed than she felt.

"HEY, WAIT TILL YOU HEAR what I found out tonight," Herb McGuire announced, as he entered The Quarter Note to relieve Megan. "Sam's real name is Sebastian and he's a classical guitarist."

"I know. His agent was in here earlier." And she'd thought about nothing else since.

"Seems like a nice enough guy. Sam—that is, Sebastian—introduced us before they took off."

"Sam's left?" *Already? Without even saying goodbye?* A knot formed in her stomach.

"They were going to do some bar hopping, I think. Sam wanted to show him Grand Rapids. Said to tell you he'd talk to you in the morning."

So Sam would be around for a little longer. But how much longer? A day? Two?

SAM'S CAR WAS GONE, the cabin dark, when Megan arrived home. She didn't want to think about him and tried to go to sleep. Sleep wouldn't come. Restlessly tossing and turning, she heard her father come in a little after two, but didn't let him know she was awake. She didn't want to talk about Sam or why she felt so empty. Not yet.

It was nearly three when she heard Sam pull the Porsche into its usual place, the car's headlights briefly illuminating the backyard before they went out. The slam of his car door was like a shot in the night. Leaving her light out,

Megan rose from her bed and went to the window to watch Sam walk to the cabin. He was whistling, and he was alone.

A breeze from the lake blew her nightgown close to her body. An icy chill ran down her spine, a cold, empty loneliness filling her heart. Megan shivered. A light went on in Sam's cabin and she stared at it, mesmerized.

His shades were drawn, but through them she could see Sam's silhouette as he moved into his bedroom. She felt like a voyeur, yet she couldn't draw her eyes away. He removed his shirt, then his trousers, his body a lean, dark shadow. She remembered their night together and yearned to reach out and touch him, to feel his warmth and security. His light went out, and a tear slid down her cheek. "Damn you," she swore, turning away from the window and walking back to her bed. "Why did you ever come here?"

THE SUN WAS just barely above the horizon when she gave up trying to sleep. Staring into the bathroom mirror, Megan didn't know whether to laugh or cry. "Face it, gal, you let him get under your skin," she told bloodshot eyes.

A hot shower helped bring some color back to her cheeks, and as she blew her short hair dry, fluffing it with her fingers to give it body, Megan decided what she was going to do.

Quickly she pulled on a pair of lacy panties, a hot-pink tank top and jeans. A touch of lipstick and some makeup helped hide the signs of her sleepless night. Her father was snoring when she tiptoed past his room, and Josh was stretched out on his bed, his sheet kicked aside, his face almost angelic as he slept. Not even bothering to put on shoes, Megan made her way to the guest cabin, the dew chilling and tickling her toes.

A mourning dove was calling when she knocked on Sam's door. He was probably asleep, but it didn't make any difference. Perversely, she reasoned that if she couldn't sleep, he shouldn't be able to, either. Again she knocked, this time louder.

"You're early, kid," Sam said through a yawn, his eyes half closed as he opened the door. "Think we could hold off on your lesson until . . . Megan?"

"I . . ." He was standing on the opposite side of the screen door wearing only a pair of white briefs, the outline of his manhood all too obvious. "I'll . . . come back later," she stammered, turning away and starting down the steps.

"Megan! No . . . wait!" He looked down at his jockey shorts and understood her reaction. "Give me just a minute to get dressed."

She turned back and stared at the door. He'd disappeared from her view, and Megan was uncertain what to do next. Logically, she should simply leave. After all, he was going to go away no matter what she said. But her legs refused to move.

In a second Sam was back, zipping up his trousers, a yellow-and-green striped polo shirt clutched in one hand. "Come on in," he said, pulling the shirt over his head, then pushing the door open for her to enter.

Megan hesitated for a moment, her eyes meeting his. Reminding herself that he had deceived her, and before he left he at least owed her the truth, she took in a deep breath and stepped forward.

As Megan entered the cabin, Sam ran his fingers through his tousled hair, trying to give his unruly blond curls some semblance of order. She was upset and he knew why. The next few minutes were going to be tricky ones, their future definitely on the line. "Coffee?" he asked, letting the screen door bang closed behind him.

"No, thank you." Megan moved to the middle of the room, then stopped and turned to face him. "So your name's Sebastian, not Sam. Sebastian Augusto?"

Her words were controlled, her attitude distant. Cautiously he answered. "Augustino. Not that that's any better. My legal name is Sebastian Augustino Blake. But my friends call me Sam."

"Classical guitarist?"

"Yes."

Suddenly the cool facade slipped, and Megan bristled. "Why didn't you tell us? How could you lie to me?"

Sam let out the breath he hadn't even realized he'd been holding. Her anger, at least, he could deal with. "I didn't lie. I am called Sam, and I told you I played the guitar."

"Played, yes," she argued, shaking her index finger at his face. "However, you neglected to mention that you're a master guitarist, an international celebrity. Dammit, Sam, you deceived us."

"No I didn't," he countered. "When I first offered to play here, there was no need for me to use the name Sebastian. You didn't need a classical guitarist at The Quarter Note, and I didn't want people coming expecting to hear one. As for my not telling you about my accomplishments, your attitude toward musicians certainly hasn't led me to believe you'd be very impressed."

"And with good reason." Her finger again rose in her defense. "You said you were different from Rod, but you're not. Maybe you play in a different ball park, but it's the same game. Fame's the name. How many people did *you* step on, Sebastian Blake?" She spat out his name.

"None," he growled, finding it difficult not to reach out and grab her by the shoulders and give her a good shake. But he knew that would only make her angrier. "Not every musician fits your little mold, Megan. There are a few of us who do play because we enjoy it. If I wanted fame, I could have had a lot more by playing the cello, or by running myself ragged accepting every offer that comes my way. But that's not what I'm after. Tell me truthfully, Megan, had you ever heard of Sebastian Blake before last night?"

"No." She eyed him suspiciously. Some of what he was saying fitted with what Cal had said in the bar. Still, she had her doubts. "But just because I haven't heard of you doesn't prove anything. Your agent said you were better known in Europe."

"All right, then—" he wondered how he was ever going to convince her that she was wrong "—would a man intent on reaching the top be content to spend a month playing at a place like The Quarter Note?"

"Good question," Megan returned. "Just why have you stayed this long?"

"Do you want my reasons listed in order?" He counted them off on his fingers. "One, because I like you. Two, because I'm enjoying playing folk songs to appreciative audiences. And, three, because you and your dad need me right now."

"Ah, yes, Sebastian the saint," she remembered. "Tell me, which do you think will rate highest? Saving a bar from going under or turning your salary over to the boys' club?"

He frowned at her question. "I'm no saint. As for the boys' club, it's one of the charities I normally support and I don't need the money you're paying me, so why shouldn't I give it to them?"

Why, indeed? He had a logical answer for everything. "Damn!" Megan turned away from him, wishing she still felt angry. She dreaded the next question she had to ask. "Did you sign that contract your agent brought?"

From behind, Megan heard his softly spoken yes, and the fight went out of her. Closing her eyes, she struggled to keep back the tears that threatened to embarrass her. "When are you leaving?"

"Do you want me to leave, Megan? Now that you know who I am, do you want me out of your life?"

"Yes!" she snapped and squeezed her lids tighter. Then she shook her head. Her back to him, her voice low and shaky, she answered. "No, of course not. Josh will miss you, and business at The Quarter Note will drop off drastically. We'll be back to third-rate musicians, and Dad will be—"

"What about you, Megan?" Sam interrupted, needing to know. "Do you want me to leave?"

A tear slipped down her cheek and touched her lips. She didn't dare brush it away or he would know she was crying.

"Megan." He repeated her name softly and stepped closer. "Turn around and face me."

Again she shook her head.

"Megan," Sam murmured and gently turned her. It was then he saw the tears. "Oh, sweet Megan."

For a moment she kept her eyes closed, then slowly opened them to find herself being looked at with so much tenderness that it made her heart ache.

"I never meant to keep anything from you," he said, brushing her tears away with the backs of his fingers. "At first I was afraid to tell you. You already seemed so set against having anything to do with a musician. Then, when I was going to say something, you said you didn't want to know anything about me. I guess I hoped that as you got to know me better, it wouldn't matter one way or the other."

"It doesn't," she whispered, her eyes locked with his. "But now I want to know. I want to know everything about you...where you were born...about your family...what you were like as a child...everything."

Sam chuckled and wrapped his arms around her, drawing her close. Lowering his head, he lightly touched his lips to hers, then paused—to see her reaction. When Megan smiled tentatively and slid her arms around his waist, he relaxed. The worst of the battle was over. Now he could be honest with her. "It's a rather long story," he said, giving her another quick kiss. "I think we'd better sit down." Taking her hand, he led her to the couch and pulled her down beside him.

"I was born in Los Angeles thirty-four years ago," he began, "and was named after my mother's father and my father." He slipped his arm around Megan's shoulders and gave her an affectionate squeeze. "Do you know there's not one decent nickname for Sebastian. My father was the one who started calling me Sam. I'm told it came from a Dr. Seuss story he used to read to me. I guess I would go around repeating 'Sam I am,' like the character in the book. To my mother's displeasure, the name stuck, but she still refuses to use it.

"My father was Augustino Blake. I don't know if you've ever heard of him. Years ago he used to compose and conduct movie scores."

"Oh, my gosh!" Megan gasped. "Of course." Why hadn't she made the connection? She'd seen the name Augustino Blake many times listed among the credits of the old movies her father loved to watch. "He won several Oscars, didn't he?"

"Seven, to be exact. He didn't do much conducting after I was born. He was in his late fifties then and not in the best of health. My mother was only twenty-five. It was her first marriage, his second. I was their only child and spoiled rotten, I'm told.

"Dad spent a lot of time with me. In his opinion, the younger a child is taught to play an instrument, the easier it will be for him, or her, to learn. By the time I was four I was playing the piano, and soon after that he started me on the violin and later, the cello. I was becoming a very good cello player, but then when I was nine he made the mistake of taking me to see Andrés Segovia. As soon as I heard that man play, I was hooked. I still remember coming home from that concert, begging for a guitar. My mother thought the instrument too unrefined, but my father finally gave in and bought me one. After that, the cello held no interest for me. I spent hours locked in my room, trying to recapture the tones I'd heard Segovia produce."

"Like Josh does," murmured Megan.

"Like Josh, only worse. My total existence suddenly revolved around that guitar. Much to mother's horror. I mean—" Sam fluttered his hand, as a woman might, and affected a falsetto "—'A guitar simply does not have class.'

"I'll tell you, my love, if you want an example of someone driven by a need for fame and recognition, it's my mother. Dad was the one who always held her in check." Sam was suddenly quiet, his expression sad. "He died when he was sixty-nine."

Megan reached up and touched his cheek. Words of sorrow, she knew, would be too empty. She'd experienced the death of a parent and knew the void it left in one's life.

"Soon after the funeral," Sam went on, "my mother decided we should move to London. Her family was originally from there and she'd always wanted to travel the Continent. My life, after that, changed dramatically."

He reached for a pack of cigarettes on the coffee table, but Megan leaned forward and put her hand over his. "Don't," she ordered softly, looking him in the eyes.

Sam paused, staring at her, then smiled and sat back. "I don't even know why I smoke them. Not that I smoke that many."

Only when you're upset or nervous, she could have told him, but she smiled instead.

Again he slid his arm around her shoulders. For a moment he was pensive, then he went on. "After my father died, my mother insisted I give up the guitar and resume my studies with the cello. It was for my own good, she claimed. I was twelve then. There was little I could do but comply. So I played the cello.

"For the next few years she managed my career as a cellist. She used the connections my father had with conductors and got me guest appearances in London and Paris. Within a year I was appearing on radio and television. There were private and public recitals. I was constantly on display." His tone was bitter.

"You must have been very good."

Sam looked at her and shrugged. "I suppose I was, but playing the cello wasn't what I wanted to do. I wanted to play the guitar."

"Then why didn't you refuse to play the cello?" As stubborn as he was now, Megan couldn't imagine Sam giving in to anyone.

"Oh, I did. Over those years it was a continuous battle. We'd argue, I'd refuse to play. I even refused to eat, once. She'd cry, cajole, make herself sick. And in the end, I'd do what she wanted." Sam absently played with a lock of Megan's dark hair. "You'll have to meet my mother someday. She's quite a manipulator. Guilt is her favorite tool. A little, 'If you loved me,' can get a lot accomplished, along with tears and an occasional dizzy spell. I was seventeen before I realized how skillfully she was handling me. That's when I took my guitar and ran away."

"What did your mother do?" His departure from the nest had nearly paralleled hers, if not for the same reasons.

"She sent the police after me, but I kept a low profile until I came of age. After that, there was nothing she could do. I had inherited some money from Dad and had the money she'd put aside for me from my performing, so I was financially independent. I resumed my study of the guitar and began building a reputation as a fairly decent player. I even managed to study with Segovia for a time.

"I'd like to say it was all easy. It wasn't. But I kept at it because it's what I loved to do . . . what I still love to do. And if I'm now considered famous, it's not because fame is something I was looking for, but something that came because others appreciated what I was doing." Sam let the tip of his fingers slide down along the side of Megan's neck and felt her shiver. Leaning closer, he grazed her cheek with his lips. "I also love kissing you."

His mouth moved closer to hers and immediately she responded, turning toward him. His kisses were messages of a fiery longing, and her answers were equally strong. Her hands moved over his shoulders in wild little circles, her fingers kneading the muscles of his arms. She wanted to touch him and to be touched . . . to be a part of him.

"Let's go into the bedroom," he rasped, voicing her feelings.

For a moment she was tempted, then remembered her son. "We can't. You know how early Josh comes over here for his lessons. We can't take a chance."

"Damn." He kissed her again, wanting so much more than her lips. Then he pulled himself back. "I think, my love, I'd better make us some coffee."

Her own heartbeat erratic, her breathing shallow, Megan nodded. "I think I need it."

Giving her a quick kiss on her forehead, Sam rose from the couch, started to pick up his cigarettes, looked at her and left the pack where it lay. With a smile, he walked to the small kitchenette. "What did you think of Cal?"

"He seemed nice enough." Shaken by the longing his kisses had awakened, Megan left the couch to walk over and lean against the counter that divided the kitchenette from the living room area. "He was worried about getting you to agree to play with the New York Philharmonic. I take it he talked you into it?"

"Cal said it was a must." Sam measured out the coffee, added cold water, then started the coffee maker. As the water began to gurgle, he turned to face her. "Cal's a good agent. I couldn't ask for better. And a good friend. He was concerned that he'd upset you last night. He didn't know I hadn't told you who I was."

"Nancy's going to give you a bad time about your name." Megan laughed, then stopped abruptly and looked down at the counter. "I forgot, you won't be playing at The Quarter Note anymore."

Sam moved to stand directly across the counter from her, his voice soothing. "Hey, Sam Blake, folk guitarist, isn't taking off yet. All that's changed is I have to start doing some serious practicing on my off hours."

"But your concert? Your five-city tour?" Her gaze met his. She didn't understand.

"That concert isn't until November, and the tour doesn't start until January. I'll have to leave sometime this fall, but not for a while." Sam reached across the counter and took her hands in his. "Did you change my work schedule?"

"I was working on it." Until Sam left, Megan wanted to spend as much time with him as she could. "What night do you want off—Sunday or Tuesday?"

"Maybe both." He leaned over and kissed her, the coffeepot gurgling behind him. "Do you have any idea how wild I am about your lips?" Little nibbles gave her some idea. "Or your cute little nose?" He planted one peck right on the end.

"My nose turns up too much," she protested, her entire body nearing the boiling point as the tip of his tongue licked a fiery path over her cheek.

"Everything about you is perfect," he murmured, tasting her tear-salted skin.

"Sam." She swallowed hard, her breathing rapidly becoming uneven.

"Yes, my love?" His warm breath blew into her hair and he gave her earlobe a playful nip.

"I think the coffee's ready." It wasn't coffee she wanted; yet, with her son apt to pop in at any time, she knew anything else would be too dangerous.

"Coffee…right." His lips touched the pulse point of her throat. "The coffee's not the only thing ready. Want to lock the door and pretend we're not here?"

"Knowing Josh, think he'll believe it?" She wished her son wasn't the persistent type.

"I think I should have followed your advice and never suggested giving him lessons." With a great deal of reluctance, Sam pulled back. "Go sit down. I'll pour."

Megan sat at the table, and Sam brought over two steaming mugs of coffee. He pulled out a chair and sat down across from her. "To a new beginning," he toasted, tapping his mug against hers.

"To a new beginning." It was strange to think of him as Sebastian Blake, classical guitarist. She'd barely gotten to know Sam Blake, the folk guitarist. "Should I call you Sam or Sebastian?"

"Sam, please. Only Cal and my mother call me Sebastian."

"Have you seen your mother since you ran away?"

"Oh, yes, many times," he said readily, sipping his coffee. "Once I'd established myself as a classical guitarist, I went back. She cried, she moaned about her delicate condition, and when I wasn't duly impressed by her performance, she ranted and raved about how I'd thrown away my chance to be a great cellist. We've now come to an understanding. She leads her life of high society without any criticism from me, and I do my own thing, without any hysterics on her part." He smiled and set down his mug. "Not that she's entirely given up on trying to manage my life. Her latest aspiration is to marry me to a duchess."

"You're not engaged or anything, are you?" She could never forgive his behavior if he was involved with another woman.

"No. I was, once, to a Spanish woman. But it didn't work out. She—"

The bang of the house's back door turned their heads at the same time. Sam chuckled. "You were right. If I'd had my way, it might have been a bit embarrassing."

"Sam," Josh called through the screen door, "I'm ready for my lesson."

8

MEGAN WENT TO BED early that night. Her lack of sleep the night before had left her exhausted, and when the telephone rang it didn't wake her as quickly as usual. It wasn't until she heard the heavy plod of her father's footsteps and the abrupt cutting off of the next ring that she became aware of her surroundings.

"Hello," Herb barked, the tone of his voice certain to intimidate any caller. "Yeah?"

She listened without being fully awake, yet immediately picked up on his attitude change. "You're sure?" he asked. "I'll be right there."

A sense of foreboding brought Megan to her feet. It was dark out, the hands of the clock barely at three-thirty. Her father was already pulling on his pants when Megan reached his room.

"What's wrong?" she demanded, watching him shove his feet into his shoes and grab for a shirt at the same time.

"That was Lyle Wilson. He says there's smoke pouring out of our place."

"Oh, no!" Megan exclaimed. Lyle Wilson lived directly across from The Quarter Note. "Should I call the fire department?"

"Lyle already did. They should be there by the time I get there." Her father poked the tail of his shirt into his pants and headed for the back door. Without even taking time to say goodbye, he rushed out of the house.

Forgetting she was wearing nothing but a nightgown, Megan ran after him. "I'm coming, too!" she yelled, then stopped as her bare feet hit the damp grass. Looking down at her skimpy attire, she changed her mind. "I'll get dressed and meet you there."

"No, stay here! I don't know what I'll find. Maybe it's only smoke."

Where there's smoke, there's fire flitted through Megan's mind, but she said nothing. Her father jerked open the door of the Volkswagen and slid in. At that moment, the fire department's sirens began to wail, shattering the stillness of the night.

The Shady Lake Fire Department consisted of two fire trucks and a staff of volunteer firemen. Always on call, they gave up their free time to train and take courses in first aid and CPR. At this hour, Megan knew, most of them would be in bed, asleep. It would take time for all of them to get to the bar.

"I'll call you as soon as I can!" her father yelled, backing out of the drive.

He drove off, and she turned and started back to the house. There was no way she was going to sit around and wait for a phone call. If she took the path near the lake, she could be at the bar in ten minutes.

"Megan, what's up?" Sam called from his window.

In the dark, she could just make out his shadowy form. "The bar!" she yelled. "It's on fire. That is, there's smoke coming out of it. Dad's gone to find out. As soon as I get dressed, I'm going, too."

"I'll take you!" he shouted, the incessant wail of the sirens nearly drowning out his words.

"Give me five minutes." She ran back into the house, stubbing her toe on one of Josh's army trucks in her rush to get to her room. "Damn," she swore, hopping on one foot and clutching her toe as she tried to find her jeans.

"Mom?" Josh called sleepily from his bedroom.

Megan grabbed a pair of old blue-and-white striped slacks. "Honey, there's a problem at the bar. Maybe a fire. I've got to go help Grampa."

"Me too." Josh stood in her bedroom door, dark hair tousled, blue eyes not yet focused.

"No, you stay here." She took the first T-shirt she found and after slipping it over her head, Megan paused to soften her abrupt refusal. "We have to have someone here to answer the telephone."

"But, Mom—" whined Josh.

"No buts—you stay here. Understood?" Megan gave him her sternest look, then hurried to put on her shoes. She didn't need to have her son in danger, as well as her father and the bar. "You'll man our checkpoint," she added, to give credence to her demand.

At that moment the telephone did ring. "Quick, go answer it. That might be Grampa," Megan ordered, tying her laces.

Josh shook his head when she approached him. "It's not Grampa," he whispered in an aside, then spoke directly into the mouthpiece. "Yeah, a fire, at the bar. Okay." He hung up. "That was Mrs. Vitteck. She heard all the yelling over here and saw the lights on, and she wondered what was going on."

"Maybe you should go next door and stay with her."

"No." Josh straightened to his full four feet eight inches. "I have to stay here and answer the telephone. Remember?"

"Right." Megan gave her son a hug, then started for the door. "I'll be back as soon as I can."

Sam was already in the Porsche, haphazardly attired, his hair in need of a comb and his eyes somewhat glazed. Megan slid in without a word, barely getting her door closed before Sam backed out of the drive and sped down the street.

That mile to the bar was the longest she'd ever traveled. Nearing The Quarter Note, Sam had to slow the car to a crawl; vehicles were coming from every direction. She could see two fire trucks in front of the bar, and all around them men were pouring out of cars and trucks, slipping into rubberized coats, pulling on their boots and picking up their yellow helmets.

Once they had their gear on, they went to work checking out the building, stretching out the hoses and readying ladders and axes. Most of the men seemed to be moving toward the back of the building. From where she sat, Megan couldn't see any flames, but thick black smoke was billowing out from under the eaves.

Sam parked the Porsche out of the way, and Megan had opened her door before he turned off the ignition. She started to run toward the front door, but Sam's long legs quickly closed the distance between them. Catching her by her wrist, he jerked her to a stop. "Where do you think you're going?" he yelled over the commotion.

"We've got to put it out!" she cried, trying to pull free from his hold.

Tightening his grasp, he kept her close. "With what— your bare hands? Let them do their job." He motioned toward the firemen.

"But I can't just stand here!" Megan shouted, feeling totally helpless. "There's got to be something we can do to help."

"All right, let's see. But stay close to me." To assure her compliance, Sam continued to hold on to her wrist as they skirted the firemen and worked their way around one fire truck toward a man giving orders through a P.A. system.

Megan recognized him as Gordon Fletcher, a neighbor and frequent customer at the bar. "Gordon, how bad is it? What can I do?" she asked, coming up beside him.

Gordon stopped talking into the transmitter he held to glance down at Megan. Recognition softened the worried lines of his face and he put a hand on her shoulder. "Megan, I'm glad you're here. You've got to keep your father out of our way. He's going to get himself hurt, going into the building the way he has been. *Get that hose over to the right!*" he yelled at a group of men in front of him.

"Where is Herb?" asked Sam.

"Last time I saw him, he was carrying a pile of books and papers over to that car." Gordon pointed to the yellow Volkswagen parked behind the second fire truck. "But one of the men said he was trying to get back inside."

"Oh, no." Megan took a step toward the building without thinking. "Dad's inside?"

Sam grabbed her wrist and held her back, as Gordon answered, "I don't know. I hope not. We don't need to be rescuing him as well as putting out this fire. *Brian, grab an ax and work with Tom!*" he instructed one of the latecomers. Then he addressed Sam. "The best thing is for all of you to stay back out of our way and let us get our job done."

"We'll stay back," Sam promised. But as he pulled Megan away from the truck, she resisted.

"Sam, let me go!" Twisting her wrist, she tried to break his hold on her arm. "If Dad's inside, I can't just stand by and do nothing."

"And what do you propose to do—go in after him? Besides the fact that you don't have any safety equipment, where are you going to look for him? You don't know where he might be. Or if he's even in there. Megan, you heard the man. He wants us out of his way. Let them do their job." Sam's fingers were strong from hours of playing the guitar, and his grip on Megan remained secure.

"But I can't just stand here." She pleaded with him with her eyes and felt his hand relax slightly.

"Then let's look for him out here."

Quickly Megan glanced around the front of the bar. There were no signs of her father. She tugged on Sam's arm and yelled, "I don't see him! Let's work our way around back!"

He nodded, the noise all around them making normal conversation impossible. Together, Sam's hand still firmly clamped around her wrist, they worked their way around the fire-fighting equipment and people, toward the back of the building.

It was obvious the worst of the fire was located near the dumpster. For the first time, Megan could see flames. Like orange tongues they were licking out of the bathroom windows, while smoke poured from every crack and crevice. Firemen were on the roof, chopping holes to give them access to the fire. "The storage room," Megan gasped.

"What about it?" asked Sam, his arms going around her in an instinctive move to protect her from the heat and smoke.

"If the fire gets to the storage room, with all those cases of liquor..." She didn't want to think what would happen. Leaning against him, Megan shuddered. "Oh, Sam, Dad's dream."

"Isn't dead yet. You have fire insurance, don't you?"

Megan nodded numbly. Her father had said they couldn't afford the cost, but she'd insisted they get some coverage on the building, at least.

"It can all be rebuilt, honey," Sam soothed, holding her close, his eyes hypnotically drawn to the flames. In front of them a drama was being played out, and they were helpless to do a thing. It was like watching the late-night news on television. Only it was real, he thought, and it was happening to them.

Megan couldn't remember how many years her dad had talked about owning his own bar. He'd scrimped and saved, and she'd felt so guilty when he'd had to use part of his savings for her maternity bills and schooling. As far as she was concerned, when she'd pooled her money with him to buy The Quarter Note she wasn't becoming a partner, she was paying back a debt.

To her father, The Quarter Note was more than just a bar; it was a part of him. After she'd agreed that they should buy it, he'd spent hours deciding on the decor and choosing the name. If he wasn't home, he was at The Quarter Note, serving drinks, talking and joking with customers, polishing glasses.

Knowing how painful this moment had to be for him, Megan resumed her search for her father. But Herb McGuire was nowhere to be seen.

Praying that she'd merely overlooked him, Megan turned away from Sam to check behind her. She could see most of the area around the back of the building and part of the front. Several people were milling about, curiosity having brought them from their warm beds to stand outside in the predawn coolness, but her father wasn't among them.

"Sam, I don't see Dad anywhere," she cried, repeating her scan of the area.

"Megan." Sam took in a deep breath, and his arm tightened around her waist.

"He's not back here and he's not—"

"Megan," he repeated, turning her toward the back door of the bar.

Her legs suddenly turned to rubber, and she leaned against Sam's strength. Eyes riveted on the back door, she held her breath. Backing out of the building was a fireman wearing an air pack, his face covered with a mask. In front of him was another fireman, also wearing an air pack and mask. And between them they were carrying the body of a man. A big, burly man, with thinning brown hair.

Megan screamed.

9

"YOU'RE LUCKY all you broke was your wrist," Megan said. She stopped scrubbing the sooty bar to face her father. "When I saw them carrying you out, I was sure you were dead."

"Might as well have been," he muttered, settling himself carefully on a bar stool.

"Dad, don't even think that."

"Food in the cooler's still all right," Pete Henshaw informed them, straightening up after checking its contents. "But with the electricity off, it won't stay that way long."

"Electricity," her father groaned. "I don't even want to hear that word." Shaking his head, he looked around the bar.

The stench of smoke was everywhere, but the main lounge had suffered no actual fire damage, and after they'd spent a day cleaning away soot and ashes, it looked a lot better than when they'd arrived that morning. Even the office was in fair shape, except for a hole in the ceiling and some water damage.

Herb's first trip into the burning building had been to save their books and business papers. Those he'd stacked safely in the car. It was the second trip that had nearly been his last.

As he told it, he'd been worried about the liquor in the storeroom. While the flames had been concentrated in the area near the bathrooms, he knew it wouldn't take long for them to spread. He hadn't been sure what he was going to do about it, and he'd never had the chance to find out.

He still couldn't say whether he'd fallen because he'd tripped or because he had been overcome by smoke. The closer he'd gotten to the back of the bar and the actual fire, the harder it had been to see and breathe. Apparently, all he remembered was coming to on the grass, an oxygen mask over his face, his wrist throbbing and his lungs and throat feeling like hell. Megan and Sam had been by his side.

"All this because of a loose wire," he grumbled. "I should have realized those blown fuses were warnings."

"The advantage of hindsight," Pete philosophized, checking the bottles along the back bar for damage. "Count yourself lucky, Herb. The place didn't burn to the ground, you have insurance and you're still alive."

"I'll drink to that," said Sam, coming through the front door at that moment, Josh by his side.

"Sam said he doesn't care what you said, we're going to help clean up," Josh announced, striding purposefully to the bar to climb up on the stool beside his grandfather. "He said it isn't right for us to sit around playing our guitars while you're all working."

"I'm certainly not doing much," Herb said, lifting his cast-covered left arm. Then he looked at Sam. "And you shouldn't feel you have to be here. In fact, you shouldn't be here. I don't want anything to happen to your hands."

"Nothing's going to happen to my hands." Sam held up his hands, examining his palms and long fingers. "They've survived thirty-four years of everyday living. I'm not about to start coddling them."

Megan loved the relaxed, easygoing way Sam handled her father. He smiled at her, and she felt a special glow deep inside. For the past two days they'd spent a lot of time together. She didn't know what she would have done without him. He'd been the calming influence when they had first carried her father out of the building. He'd gone with her to the hospital and stood by her side while she waited for the doctor's report. And when they knew her father would be fine, that the worst he had suffered was a broken wrist and sore ribs from all his coughing, Sam had been the one who had driven them home. Then he'd taken Josh away with him so her father and she could get some sleep.

"You've done enough already," she said. "Believe me, this is dirty work."

Sam grinned. Megan's face and arms were smudged with soot, her T-shirt and jeans soiled from rubbing against charred wood. "I believe you. Why are you cleaning up, anyway? Won't your insurance company take care of that?"

Both Megan and her father shook their heads. "We probably have the most basic policy ever written," Megan explained. "They'll pay for the replacement of the fire-damaged area and our damaged stock, but that's it. We just didn't have enough money to get anything more comprehensive."

"A lack of money is exactly what got us into this mess," Herb went on. "If we'd had more money, I not only would have gotten a better policy, I'd have also had this place re-wired and put in a sprinkling system. But we didn't have any money after we bought it, and from the looks of this place we never will."

"We'll get The Quarter Note open again," Megan assured him. "It'll just take a little elbow grease and time." She was concerned about her father's attitude. Since the fire he'd been depressed. "You heard the insurance man yourself. He said he'd start processing our claim immediately. Once we get the money, we can rebuild."

"Once we get the money," Herb repeated sarcastically. "It'll be winter by the time they pay us and we have the work done and our supplies restocked...maybe even spring. We'll have lost months of business, as well as most of our customers. We might as well chauffeur them over to the other bar. They won't be coming back here."

Leisurely Sam wandered toward the back of the building where the firefighters had chopped a gaping hole in the wall. Above him the sun shone through charred rafters. "If a crew got started right away, they could have the damage cleared away and a new section up in less than a month."

"It all comes back to that matter of money," Herb said bitterly. "I'll bet it'll be at least a month before the insurance agency company even finishes the paperwork."

"Really?" Sam turned his head to look back at them.

Herb McGuire nodded, his gray eyes clouded, his posture weary and defeated. "This company is known for its low premiums, not its speedy payments."

"Let's go for a walk, Herb," Sam suggested, motioning for him to come. "You look like you need a bit of fresh air."

"Might as well. Can't do anything here." Herb shrugged and slid off the stool. Slowly he made his way toward Sam, the spring to his walk completely gone.

Megan was glad Sam was getting her father out of the bar. Ever since they'd arrived, all he'd done was mope around. In part she blamed his lassitude on the painkillers the doctor had prescribed for his arm, but she also knew a good deal of his pain was not physical. The fire had damaged more than a building.

"Can I play the piano?" begged Josh.

"Go ahead," Megan replied absently, watching her father and Sam step over the rubble and go out through the hole that was once a wall.

It was difficult not to let depressive feelings invade her own psyche. She knew Sam would be leaving now. With no bar, there was no reason for Sam Blake the folk guitarist to stay. Sebastian Blake would be returning to New York.

She tried to rationalize that perhaps this was all for the best. If he left now she'd have a lot to keep her busy, and she wouldn't miss him so much.

But she knew it was going to be painful, no matter how busy she was. She couldn't put into words how she felt about Sam. She definitely liked him. In fact, she'd go as far as to say she felt a strong affection for him. No, the word "affection" didn't really describe how she felt, either.

Megan wouldn't let her thoughts go on. Almost violently she attacked the countertop with a soapy sponge, scrubbing vigorously to remove all traces of soot before rinsing the wood and drying it with a towel. As she worked she questioned Pete about the condition of the stock he was taking inventory of, and made mental notes of what they would need to reorder.

For a long time she wasn't really aware of Josh's piano playing. He would hit one note, then another; there would be a pause, then he'd try again. She wasn't sure when the notes stopped being random selections and started to fit together. It wasn't until Pete spoke up that she actually stopped and listened.

"Sounds like you're going to have quite a piano player there. When did you start giving him lessons?"

"Josh?" Megan put down the sponge and stared at her son.

Seated on the piano stool, his toes just barely touching the floor, Josh had found some sheet music and was picking out the melody of "Those Lazy Hazy Crazy Days of Summer."

She stepped out from behind the bar to cross the room and stand beside her son. How she didn't know, but it was obvious Josh was reading the music. He was only using his right hand to play, but it did sound like the song.

In fact, it sounded darned good, she thought. "When did you learn that?" Megan asked, wondering if Sam had brought Josh to the bar sometime and taught him.

"Just now," Josh said proudly, turning to look up and grin. "Except I don't know how to play these." He pointed to the chords.

"You taught yourself?" Megan found that difficult to believe. Josh had been to the bar before, when it was closed. While he'd often played on the piano during those visits, he'd merely banged away on the keys, the sounds in no way creating what she would have called music.

"Well, I found out where this was on the piano." He pointed to middle C and played the corresponding key. "After that, it was easy."

"I told you he's talented," Sam said, coming up behind her. "One of these days I'll teach you how to play chords on a piano," he told Josh. "It's not hard to learn."

"I can't believe learning to play the guitar has taught him how to play the piano." Megan shook her head in amazement.

"Not many kids could make the transition." Reaching past her, Sam tousled Josh's hair. "The maestro here is an exception."

Josh beamed and Megan stared at her son. Although she was proud of Josh, an icy dread was creeping through her. Sam had told her not to compare Josh to his father, but it was impossible not to do so. Would Josh also quit school in the tenth grade, as Rod had? Would jamming with his friends and getting a gig become more important than getting an education? The possibility frightened her.

"Megan," her father interrupted her thoughts, "have you heard one thing I said?"

"No." She shook her head, surprised by the smile on her father's face. He'd come up beside Sam, and his entire attitude seemed changed. "What did you say?"

"I've decided to take out a loan. Why let that bar on the other side of the lake take away all our business? We know we're getting the insurance money, the agent said there'd be no problem and we could go ahead and get the estimates. Once we know what it's going to cost, we can simply take out a loan. That way we can have the burned part of the building torn down and the repairs done by the end of August."

"Will the bank give us a loan?" she questioned.

With a smile of certainty, her father nodded. "No problem. The Quarter Note will be back in business in no time. So what do you say we call it quits for the day?"

"You can," she said, not quite as optimistic as her father about a bank lending them money. Even with the promise of an insurance payment, their financial situation simply wasn't that strong. "I want to finish cleaning the counter."

"But I was going to take everyone out for an ice cream. You too, Pete," Herb called back to the older man. "Least I can offer, with you volunteering to help."

"Make that a chocolate shake and you're on," said Pete, pulling off his soiled apron and coming out from behind the bar.

Megan shook her head. She didn't want to dampen her father's enthusiasm with her concerns. With the prospect of reopening in a month, his spirits had risen dramatically. "You go on without me. I'm not in the mood for an ice cream, and it won't take me long to finish up here. I'll just walk home after I'm done."

"You're sure?" her father persisted, unwilling to give up until he was certain he couldn't change her mind. "You've already put in a full day's work."

"I'm sure."

"All right, then. See you later." He gave her a one-armed hug and a peck on her cheek. "And don't worry, hon. Things are going to be just like before. Even better. You wait and see."

All three men and Josh left The Quarter Note together. In their wake came silence. A towel still in one hand, Megan looked around the bar and felt tears sting her eyes. Chewing on her lower lip, she tried not to cry.

How could things be just like before? Sam wouldn't be around. Absently she wiped the towel over the stool he always used, the cloth immediately turning black. Closing her eyes, she could picture him sitting there, his guitar at an angle in front of him, the heel of his left boot hooked over the rung, his right leg stretched out. How she loved his music. How she— "Penny for your thoughts." Sam's deep voice came from behind her.

"Oh!" She spun around to face him, her eyes snapping open. "I thought you'd left."

"I decided to stay and help you." He reached forward and touched a smudge of soot on the tip of her nose, then let his fingertips travel to the smooth curve of her cheek. "I missed being around you today."

"I missed you, too," she admitted. He looked so darn sexy. Her eyes drifted down, over his blue T-shirt to his tight fitting denims. Then, realizing the direction of her gaze, Megan jerked her head up and laughed. "I think you stayed to distract me."

"Not a bad idea." Sam smiled and stepped closer. "Not a bad idea at all."

"I've got to finish the counter on the front bar," she reminded him.

"And with my help, the job will take only half the time." A quirk of his eyebrows suggested Sam had plans for the other half of her time.

Butterflies invaded Megan's stomach. "You really shouldn't be here," she murmured and took his hand in hers, bringing his fingers to her lips. Lightly she kissed them. "Dad's right—if anything should happen to your hands..."

"I'll be careful." The blue of his eyes deepened to a rich lapis azure. "Everything's going to be all right. Trust me."

"I do," she murmured, and realized she did.

Sam slid his arms around her, drawing her close. "Oh, Megan." Then he kissed her—lovingly and longingly.

His lips moved with abandon over hers, and Megan opened her mouth, inviting his tongue to enter. He accepted the invitation and at the same time found the softness of her breasts. Still kissing her, he moved one hand up under her T-shirt.

His breathing was becoming uneven, and Megan forgot about soot and dirt. Instead, her thoughts centered on the hot rush of blood that spread through her arteries the moment his lips met hers, the aching in her loins and the heady sensation of being desired. Even the reality of his leaving didn't matter. At the moment, all she knew was that she wanted him.

She tried to think of a place in the bar where they could go, then realized the foolishness of that idea. With the hole in the wall, people had been curiously wandering in and out all day long. "Sam," Megan gasped, pulling back, "someone might walk in."

He stared at the gaping opening at the back of the building, then looked down at his hand, still under the T-shirt. "My place?"

"The counter..." she began, immediately glancing over at the bar. Then she laughed, giddy with her need for him. "The counter can wait."

"And I'll help you—later," he promised. "Let's go."

They were nearly to the front door when it opened and her father entered, calling out their names. "Hey, Pete just invited us to his grandson's little league baseball game tonight. Want to go? He'll drive."

"Tonight?" asked Megan, shaken by her father's sudden appearance. A flush of color flooded her cheeks. She was certain anyone who saw them would know what they'd been doing—what they were planning to do.

"Yeah. The game's in Grand Rapids. Play-offs for some title. Afterward there's a hot dog roast. Josh wants to go," her father explained. "You're invited, too, Sam."

As she groped for a reason not to go, Megan looked at Sam, wondering what he would say.

"Not tonight, Herb," Sam refused easily.

"Me, either," she added a bit too quickly. "As soon as I finish here, I think I'll take a bath and curl up with a good book."

The rise of her father's thick eyebrows told her he didn't believe her. Suspiciously his gaze moved from her face to Sam's. "One of the classics, right?"

She tried to sound completely innocent. "Actually, it's a mystery I picked up last week. You and Josh go on and have a good time. See you when you get back."

"Right." Again Herb's glance moved between them, then a smile curved his lips. "Don't wait up for us. We may be out quite late."

It wasn't until after her father had left that Megan realized she was holding Sam's hand. "I don't think he believed me." She laughed self-consciously. "And I think I'd better finish that counter or it's going to be quite obvious I was lying."

"Nothing like the unexpected arrival of a parent to cool one's ardor. Right?" Sam followed her to the bar.

"It's silly, I know," Megan tried to explain, picking up the sponge she'd been using and starting on the last quarter of the counter. "I'm a grown woman. If I want to have an affair, it's my decision." She laughed at her own embarrassment. "I guess under some circumstances one never ceases to be a child."

Sam grabbed another sponge and followed her strokes with a clean rinse. "Does that mean you've changed your mind?"

Megan paused to look at him. He looked so crestfallen that she had to smile—he was so dear. "Let's hurry up and finish here," she said with a grin. "I need to take that bath and get involved with a classic."

STANDING IN FRONT of the vanity mirror, Megan had to laugh. There was dirt on her forehead, her nose and her chin. "Sam, what you see in this face is beyond me." She spoke aloud to her reflection.

A quick shower washed off the soot and grime and when she stepped out of the bathroom, she felt refreshed and alive. Standing in front of her closet, only a towel covering her damp torso, she pondered what to wear.

It had taken them an hour to finish cleaning the counter. There had been no more heated kisses, the job at hand occupying their time, but as they left the bar, Sam had invited her to dinner, saying he had two steaks in the freezer. She'd accepted, saying steak sounded better than a can of soup, but they both knew why she was going to the cabin. Megan pulled a blue cotton sundress from its hanger.

She dusted her body with a lightly scented powder, then pulled on lacy panties. A bra and slip seemed a waste of time, so she left them off. The cotton dress revealed little, yet its scooped neck and fitted waist enhanced her figure. And the color was perfect. Blue always brought out the gray of her eyes and the darker tones of her hair.

She kept her makeup simple—just enough to accent her eyes. Slipping on a pair of sandals and running her fingers through her already dry hair, she took one last look in the mirror and decided she was ready.

She knocked on the screen door, and Sam called for her to come in. He was in the kitchenette, opening a bottle of wine, when she entered the cabin. He looked up and smiled. "Perfect timing," he said, as the cork came out with a little *pop*.

From the dampness of his curls, Megan knew he'd also taken a shower. Dressed in shorts and a loose-weave sports shirt, he didn't look like a world-famous guitarist. Even less so when he stepped from behind the counter, carrying two glasses of wine and not wearing any shoes.

"To The Quarter Note," he toasted, handing her one glass, then raising his to tap against hers. "And to our future."

"To our future," she repeated, silently adding, *for however long that is*. She'd promised herself not to think about his leaving, to enjoy every minute they had together, but it was difficult to keep the thought from her mind.

"Hungry?"

"Starved." She smiled and sipped her wine, determined not to let anything ruin the evening.

"Good, so am I." Sam guided her to the kitchenette. Two steaks lay on the counter, still partially frozen, beside a head of lettuce and two tomatoes. "Not much, but it will have to do. Unless you'd rather go out to dinner?" He looked at her for an answer.

Setting her wineglass down by the sink, Megan reached for the lettuce. "Looks fine to me. I'll fix the salad."

They worked side by side, talking and laughing. In no time at all, the food was ready. And twenty minutes later, Megan was setting down her fork.

"I can't believe I ate the whole thing." She laughed at herself. Nothing had interfered with her appetite this evening. Only a few scraps of meat and a bit of salad were left on her plate. Feeling very contented, she sipped the last of her wine.

"You should have been hungry. You put in a full day's work today. Hard, dirty work." Sam pushed aside his own empty plate. "Let's go over to the couch and relax."

"But the dishes . . ." protested Megan, as Sam rose from his chair.

"Will wait." He extended his hand and she took it, rising to her feet and walking with him to the couch.

Megan sat close to Sam, who slid his arm behind her shoulders. She leaned her head back and closed her eyes. For a while they said nothing, the silence between them comfortable, the singing of crickets outside the window creating a musical background. Then Sam asked, "How late do you think your dad and Josh will be out?"

"I don't know. Ten? Eleven?" Megan hoped her father was having a good time. She'd been so glad to see him in high spirits. After the past few days of moping, it was a pleasant change. Turning her head, she looked at Sam. "Did you suggest Dad get a loan?"

"I mentioned the idea."

"I hate to be a wet blanket, but I can't imagine any bank giving us money."

Sam kissed her cheek lightly and squeezed her shoulders. "Stop worrying. Your dad will get the money he needs."

"I don't—" she began, but his finger on her lips stopped her.

"Trust me," he insisted. "You're not to worry about money. Not tonight and not tomorrow."

Megan smiled and kissed his fingertip. "Oh, Sam, you make it all sound so easy. What am I going to do when you leave?"

"Maybe come with me?"

"Sure, take off tomorrow and leave Dad with a half-burned bar, a twenty-year mortgage and no one to take care of him." The idea was too farfetched to take seriously.

"I'm not leaving tomorrow, Meg," Sam assured her.

"Well, maybe not tomorrow," she amended, "but you'll be leaving soon. There's no reason for you to stay now that The Quarter Note's closed."

"Oh, I don't know about that." His words weren't much more than a whisper as he feathered a kiss over her temple. "Josh says there are still plenty of fish in that lake."

In spite of her sorrow, Megan laughed. "Sam, I swear I've eaten more fish this summer than ever before in my life."

"Doctor says they're good for you." His lips brushed her forehead. "Want to play doctor?"

"Sam?" Her pulse was racing and she turned slightly to face him. "About your leaving—"

"Did I ever tell you what a cute little nose you have?" He kissed her nose.

"You're avoiding the subject." Her eyes were on his. "How much longer?"

"Before I make love to you?"

His tone was suggestive, and Megan's heart skipped a beat. "Before you leave."

"You're always trying to get rid of me." His lips were nearing her mouth.

"I—" Spellbinding blue eyes held her captive. When he would leave lost all meaning. Here. Now. That was what was important. Megan reached up and combed her fingers into thick, golden curls. "Sam." She couldn't stand it any longer. "Kiss me."

"I thought you'd never ask." Masterfully his mouth touched hers, expressing his devotion far better than words. And, in harmony, her lips moved with his.

She welcomed the thrust of his tongue, teasingly caught it between her teeth, then set it free. One kiss led to another, then another, and another. Strong, sensitive hands moved over her back, along her sides and to her hips. Her skin warmed to his touch, her temperature soaring until the room felt oppressively hot.

"Let's go into the bedroom where it's cooler," Sam suggested, his own body damp with perspiration.

"Cooler?" Megan couldn't help but grin. The way Sam made her feel, no room was going to be cooler.

But the bedroom did have a ceiling fan, which Sam quickly turned on. He pulled the shade and the room took on a cozy, shadowy glow. "Better?" he asked, coming back to stand in front of her.

"That depends on your definition of better." Megan wrapped her arms around his neck. "Have you cooled down?"

He chuckled suggestively and drew her hips against his. "What do you think?"

His arousal was an undeniable fact. "You do feel quite warm. Maybe you should take your shirt off."

"Hmm," he murmured, leaning close to nibble on her neck. "Actually it was your dress I was thinking we should remove."

Reaching behind her, he loosened the zipper and her dress slipped from her shoulders to fall in a soft blue pool around her ankles. She was in his arms, wearing nothing but panties and sandals, but her skin felt no cooler. Instead a fiery longing raised her temperature to dangerous heights, and her legs felt weak and rubbery.

"Beautiful," he muttered, gazing down at the milky white breasts pressed against his shirt.

"Now your shirt?"

He released her briefly, pulling his shirt over his head and letting it drop to the floor beside her dress. Then he wrapped his arms around her, drawing her up on her toes and pressing her nipples against the hard wall of his chest. "Oh, Megan," he murmured reverently, his lips seeking hers.

She craved the hungry way he kissed her, as though he could never get enough. And the way he touched her, his hands so strong yet gentle. She couldn't help but respond to his caresses, her own hands moving up to his neck, then down his back to his hips. "Touch me," he begged, and she did, wanting to give him as much pleasure as he was giving her.

His shorts came off next, along with his underpants, but when she reached out to touch him again he stopped her. "No, not yet," he said, his voice none too steady. "Not unless you want this over before we start."

He kneeled before her and began to unbuckle the straps of her sandals, and Megan trembled with anticipation. Her shoes off, he reached up and let his fingertips move over the silky nylon of her panties and heard her intake of breath. Teasingly he traced the outline of the waistband, then the elastic around each leg. His fingers strayed between her legs and she groaned. The throbbing ache in his own loins urged him on, and he stopped his teasing and finished undressing her.

As one they moved to the bed, Sam gently lowering her onto the spread, then lying beside her. His kisses were demanding, his hands seductive as they roamed over her body, renewing their familiarity with the spots that gave her the most pleasure. "Oh, Sam," she sighed, her entire body turning to quicksilver. "I want you."

"And I want you." In fact, his need for her was growing stronger every minute, and he wondered how long he could control his desire. Expertly he stroked her, wanting to be certain she was ready for him, that nothing would mar their union. She trembled under his touch and he knew that neither of them could wait any longer.

Angling his body over hers, he rested his hands on either side of her and brought his mouth down gently. "I love you," he said, his lips a hairbreadth from hers. And then he was a part of her.

10

MEGAN STARTED TO ROLL OVER, then stopped. Her hand had touched a body. A warm, naked body. Her eyes flew open and she was staring into orbs of iridescent blue. "Oh, no," she groaned.

"Hi." Sam grinned and brushed her cheek with his fingertips. "Sleep well?"

"It's . . . it's morning." Megan stammered the obvious, noting the sunlight forcing its way through the drawn shade.

"It certainly is," he agreed and leaned closer to kiss her.

"But you don't understand." She held him back, looking around the room for a clock. "It's eight-thirty! Dad and Josh are bound to be up by now."

She hadn't planned on spending the night with Sam. After their initial lovemaking, they'd gotten dressed and returned to the kitchenette to wash the dishes. Afterward, Sam had made coffee and they'd sat on the couch and talked. Not really about anything, and yet, about everything. She'd felt so comfortable, curled up beside him, her feet on the cushion, her head resting on his shoulder and his arm wrapped around her. She'd planned on being home before her dad and Josh returned; yet when Sam had taken her hand and led her back to the bedroom, she hadn't objected.

Looking over the edge of the bed, Megan saw her blue dress lying in a heap, Sam's shorts beside it. "What is my father going to say?" She sank back on the pillow and covered her eyes with her hand. "How am I going to explain this to Josh?"

"You could tell them that that mystery you were reading scared you so much you ran over here for protection, and I willingly sacrificed a night of sleep to soothe you."

"Sam, be serious," Megan chided. "Maybe they don't know I'm not there yet. Maybe I can crawl through my bedroom window and—"

The telephone rang and Sam reached across her to answer it, his chest brushing the sheet and pressing the soft cotton against her bare breasts. "Hello?" he answered cautiously, then laughed. "Sure, Herb, I'll ask her. Fifteen minutes?" He covered the mouthpiece with his hand. "Can you be ready for breakfast in fifteen minutes, and how many eggs do you want?"

Megan slid down under the sheet, then she, too, began to laugh. "I guess there's no use trying to sneak in. Tell him to give me half an hour, at least. And two eggs. I'm starved."

"Caught in the act." Megan chuckled, watching Sam hang up the receiver. "Good morning." She wrapped her arms around his neck, stopping him from moving back to his side of the bed.

"Good morning, my love." He gave her a quick kiss and rolled his body on top of hers.

"Sam," she said seriously. "I know you always call me your love, but last night . . ."

"What?"

"Oh, nothing."

"Nothing?" He levered himself up slightly to get a better look at her face. He was certain he knew what she was talking about. At the height of passion, the words had slipped out before he could stop them, and he wasn't really sure what her reaction had been.

"Nothing." Now she wished she'd never brought up the subject. With a false little laugh, she tried to pass it off. "We probably both said a lot of things last night that we didn't mean."

Sam frowned down at her, his gaze a steely blue. "Last night I told you I love you, Megan. I meant it."

Her laughter died and she stared at his craggy face. Maybe he wasn't the man she would have picked, and it was probably all wrong, but she knew what it was she felt for him. It was more than admiration or liking. So much more. She loved him. Completely and unconditionally.

Reaching up she touched the pale stubble of beard on his cheek. "Crazy," she finally murmured. "This is all so crazy. You . . . a musician, of all people."

"Megan, I—"

She stopped him, her small hand covering his mouth. "You said you'd change my mind about musicians." The smile that curved her lips reached her eyes. "Well, you did. At least you changed my mind about one musician. Sebastian Augustino Blake, I love you, too."

Hugging her close, Sam burrowed his face in the hollow of her neck. "You just made me one very happy man."

They kissed, but then the impact of what she had said—what he had said—hit her. "Oh, Sam, what are we going to do?" She could see no future for them. Perhaps he wasn't striving after fame as Rod had, but he did have his career. He couldn't give that up to live in Shady Lake; she would never ask that of him. And she couldn't leave. Not while her father still needed her.

"We're going to be very happy. That's what we're going to do." And his mouth covered hers again.

With his lips playing over hers, worries about the future seemed mundane. Teasingly she rotated her hips against his and heard the groan that came from deep within his chest. He hardened against her and her own body responded. "We should have told your father we'd be longer than half an hour," Sam muttered, forcing himself away from her.

Megan held him so he couldn't leave. "I'm quite sure Dad knows what we've been doing. Our being a little late isn't going to surprise him. As for Josh, he's going to have too many questions no matter when we arrive. So...it all comes down to, do you really care if your breakfast is a little cold?" She arched against him and grinned.

IT WAS AN HOUR before they entered the kitchen, their faces slightly flushed, their hair still damp from the shower they'd shared, and her blue dress wrinkled. "About time," her father griped, looking up from his cup of coffee. "Your eggs are in the oven. Hard as leather, I'm sure."

"Sorry. It took a little longer than we'd expected," Megan apologized. She opened the oven door and removed the platter of eggs and pancakes. "They look great."

"Hrump," was all her father said.

"Mom!" Josh cried, running in from the living room, where he'd been watching television. "Where have you been?"

"I—" she began, but stopped, sharing a silent communication with Sam.

Slipping his arm possessively around her shoulders, he drew her close. "She spent the night with me, Josh. I love your mother, and I wanted to be with her."

Herb McGuire smiled and leaned back in his chair. Josh stared at Sam for a moment, then at his mother. Finally he looked back at Sam. "Is she going to stay with you all the time?"

Caressing the side of her arm, Sam gazed down at Megan. "No, not all the time. But I would like to take her on a little trip, if that's all right with you two."

"Where?" Megan, her father and Josh asked in unison.

Sam directed his answer primarily to her father. "You won't need either of us for a few days . . . not until the construction work is finished. I thought Megan and I might go to Lake Michigan, maybe drive north, along the shoreline. I hear it's a pretty trip."

"You'll want to see Holland and Sleeping Bear Dune," said her father, picking up on the idea. "Yes, that's a great idea. Meg hasn't had a vacation for years. It would do her good."

"Dad, I can't just take off!" exclaimed Megan, surprised by her father's willing acceptance.

"Can I go, too?" pleaded Josh.

"Not this time, son." Sam reached out for the boy and brought him closer. "Your mom and I need to get to know each other a little better. Next time we'll take you."

"When?" asked Josh, more concerned about his turn than about his mother taking off with Sam.

"Sam, this is ridiculous. I can't go," Megan persisted.

"Of course you can go," her father said. "Josh and I will be fine, won't we, Josh. This will give us some man-to-man time." He grinned at his grandson, and Josh nodded vigorously.

"But your arm—"

"Is no problem. What I can't do, Josh can." He looked at Sam. "How long will you be gone?"

"A week all right with you?" Sam inquired.

"Perfect."

"You're not listening to me," Megan cried, shrugging Sam's arm off her shoulders and stepping away so she could face both men. "I'm not going."

THEY LEFT AT FOUR O'CLOCK, the Porsche loaded down with two suitcases, a guitar, drawing materials and a sketch pad. The latter two items had been Sam's idea. "I'll have to practice every day. You'll need something to occupy your time," he'd explained.

How she'd been talked into going, Megan wasn't really sure, but she'd found it increasingly difficult to say no with her son begging her to leave so he and Grampa could rough it, and her father insisting he didn't need her around. And the more she thought about spending seven days with Sam, the more appealing the idea became.

"First stop, Holland, Michigan," Sam announced, heading west.

"Tulip center of America," Megan added.

"I played in Holland once. Amsterdam. Very appreciative audience." He smiled at her. "I'm glad you decided to come."

"So am I, now." Leaning back in the seat, she gazed at his profile. Seven days. She wondered if she'd love him more or less by the end of the week.

Though Holland's millions of tulips weren't blooming in August, windmills and manicured gardens, wooden shoe factories and canals still gave the town a distinctive Dutch atmosphere. Megan and Sam checked into a motel as soon as they arrived, swam in the pool, then had dinner in a downtown restaurant. It was still early in the evening when they returned to their room, a king-size bed having beckoned them back. Locked away from a world of cares and worries, they forgot everything but each other.

And when they awoke the next morning, it didn't matter that the sun was high in the sky. Time no longer ruled their days. After a leisurely breakfast, they headed for Windmill Island. "Two minutes and two centuries from downtown," Megan read from the brochure in her hand. In fact, the two-hundred-year-old windmill, De Zwann, that was the main feature of the park, was clearly visible from the parking area where they sat.

They visited the windmill first, climbing the steep wooden stairs in the wake of a Dutch-costumed tour guide. "In the 1700s windmills dotted the Netherlands countryside like oil derricks do today in the American southwest," the man said by rote, while Megan tried not to giggle. Unseen by the guide or the other tourist couple ahead, Sam was dotting her behind with little love pats.

The somber guide went on and on. The other couple listened intently and nodded their heads now and then, but Megan could hardly concentrate on what was being said and wished she'd worn more than a pair of shorts and a halter top. She had too much flesh revealed, and Sam was enjoying every inch of it.

They stepped out from the dark interior, onto an open catwalk that surrounded the windmill. It was over four stories high, and Megan stood back from the railing and shivered. But the goose bumps that covered her body had little to do with her fear of heights or the temperature, which was well into the eighties. It was Sam. He stood behind her, provocatively running his fingertips over her bare skin and creeping closer to her breasts, all the while seeming to be innocently looking out over the park.

"Stop!" she whispered, the word coming out louder than she expected.

The tour guide immediately stopped his spiel and looked her way. "You have a question?"

The couple in front of her turned to stare, and Sam grinned, his hands now discreetly by his sides.

Color flooded her cheeks, and Megan looked down at the canal that separated the windmill from the rest of the park. What could she ask? "Where did the canal come from?"

She knew it was a stupid question, but it was the best she could come up with on short notice. The guide's patient answer did little to ease her embarrassment. "It was built here, in Michigan, to reclaim the area of the floodplain along the Black River. Without the canals, this would be swampland."

"Sebastian Blake, when I get my hands on you—" Megan threatened in a hushed voice.

"Yes?" Sam's tone was suggestive.

"You're a dirty old man."

"And you're too tempting to resist." His arm went around her shoulders when the tour reached the bottom floor. "Want to see a movie about windmills?"

The way he said it, Sam might have been inviting her to view his etchings, and Megan couldn't help but laugh. "Sit in a dark room with you?" she asked under her breath so the others couldn't hear. "You've got to be kidding."

Both laughing, they left the windmill and strolled hand in hand past the authentic old Dutch carousel and mechanized miniature model of Old Holland. *Klompen* dances were being performed by girls dressed in folk costumes and wooden shoes, and they paused to watch. Moving on to the souvenir shop, Megan bought a pair of wooden shoes for Josh, while Sam picked out a blue-and-white glazed delftware bell for her father. "So he can ring when breakfast is ready."

"Would you have heard a bell ringing yesterday morning?" teased Megan.

"I did hear bells ringing." He kissed her cheek. "Didn't you?"

"You're crazy." She giggled, happier than she had been in years. "And I think I am, too."

"Wouldn't have it any other way."

By the time they returned to their motel room, Megan was exhausted. "I feel like I walked a hundred miles today."

"I think we did," Sam agreed, setting down their packages and slipping off his shoes. He stretched out on the bed and reached for his guitar case. "Why don't you take a long, hot bath?"

"Sounds like a heavenly idea."

Stretching her legs, she watched him unlatch the case and remove his guitar. He stroked each string in rapid succession, then turned a peg to correct the tension on one, bringing it into tune. As soon as he was satisfied with the sound, he played the scales to warm up his fingers. The speed and clarity of his strokes amazed Megan. "It must have taken a lot of practice to get that fast," she commented.

"Five to six hours a day. Sometimes longer if I'm learning a new piece."

"And you taught yourself?"

"In part." He hit a chord, then another, changing from the major to the minor scales. "Before I had a chance to work with Segovia, I studied on my own, first learning the works by Sor and Tárrega."

Realizing the names probably meant nothing to her, Sam explained. "Sor has often been called the Beethoven of the guitar and Tárrega was the early twentieth-century concert guitarist who inspired a whole generation of players, including Andrés Segovia. And, of course, Segovia is the man who changed the guitar from 'an instrument not worth cultivating', as my mother would say, to a popular and acceptable one."

Megan sat on the end of the bed, fascinated by his adroit playing, as well as by what he was saying.

"Segovia told me once that the guitar is the ideal instrument to carry on a dialogue with the woman you love." As if to emphasize his words, he began to play a lilting love song.

"Guitar players owe him a lot. Besides transcribing works by the great masters like Beethoven and Bach for the guitar, he solicited works from contemporary composers, so that today there's a large collection of classical pieces for the guitar. And a long list of great classical guitarists—Christopher Parkening, Julian Bream, John Williams, Liona Boyd . . ."

"And Sebastian Blake?" She ran her fingernail down the insole of his foot and grinned as he jerked his leg back in a reflex action.

"I like to think so." With a quick strum, he finished the song, moved the guitar off his lap and leaned it against the nightstand.

The next thing Megan knew, she was being pinned against the bedspread, a blond head was burrowing into her shoulder and quicksilver fingers were tickling her ribs. "Sam, stop that!" She tried halfheartedly to push him away. "Sam, please." She wriggled beneath him, her hips rubbing against his.

"All day long you've been tempting me with this beautiful body of yours."

"I didn't mean—"

Her words were cut off by the touch of his lips. Tickling fingers became caressing hands. "I love your body," he murmured over her mouth. "I love everything about you."

"And I love you," Megan sighed, all fight going out of her.

The guitar was forgotten, along with her bath and her tired legs. Clothes were discarded, two bodies in their natural state touching—the tan of his arms a contrast to the white of her hips. Nothing was rushed. Sweet kisses spoke of their love and then grew more impassioned; exploring hands found rich treasures.

Together they soared to the heights and shared the ecstasy. When it was over they lay in each other's arms, tired but satisfied, and the world seemed in perfect harmony. There was no tomorrow, only the moment. Sebastian Blake was simply Sam, and Megan refused to let herself think of anything that might mar the happiness that filled her heart.

IN THE MORNING they drove north. Taking their time, they followed the Lake Michigan shoreline, past Grand Haven, Muskegon and Ludington, on up to Manistee and Frankfort. Finally, at Glen Haven, not far from the Sleeping Bear Dune, they found a place to stay.

It was a modern housekeeping cottage, with a private beach and swimming area, sailing facilities, tennis courts and all the solitude they desired. Sam took a shower while Megan called her father. "Everything's fine back at Shady Lake," she told Sam, as he stepped out of the bathroom, a towel wrapped around his waist, his hair hanging in wet ringlets. "Dad said to tell you he had no trouble getting the money, and a construction company is scheduled to start work Monday."

"Great." Sam sat on the edge of the bed next to her and reached over to unbutton her blouse.

"Josh sounded a little envious when I told him we might go sailing tomorrow," Megan went on, helping Sam by slipping her arms out of the sleeves.

"We'll have to take him with us next time." The clasp of her bra opened easily.

"Next time?" she teased coyly, falling back against the pillows. "Aren't you getting pretty sure of yourself, Mr. Blake? Maybe I'll have grown bored with you after a week of lovemaking."

"Think so?" He traced the outline of her breasts with the tips of his fingers and watched her expression.

She couldn't help laughing as his fingers strayed to her ribs. In just three days he'd discovered the places to touch that tickled her, the places that relaxed her and the places that gave her the most pleasure. "No, I don't think I'd ever get bored with you," she admitted, almost frightened by that realization.

"Of course not." He unbuttoned her slacks and pulled them off. "'Cause I'm a lovable guy." Wrapping his arms around her, he twisted his body and ended up lying on his back, with her sprawled across him.

"Insatiable, I think would be a better word," Megan said with a smile. "I thought we were getting ready to go to dinner."

"Are you hungry?" he asked, nibbling on her neck in a way that raised goose bumps on her arms.

"Not really." She laughed and did a little nibbling of her own on his shoulder. "At least not for food."

IN THE MORNING they strolled along the shoreline. Lake Michigan extended as far as they could see, the wind whipping enormous waves against the sand, as the dark gray clouds above turned the water a murky green color. "Didn't the weatherman know we'd planned on going sailing?" Megan groaned, hearing the distant rumble of thunder.

"I bribed him so I could keep you in the cottage all day." Sam leered.

"You're going to have to catch me if you want me." She freed her fingers from his and took off at a run.

Megan knew she couldn't outrun Sam, but escape wasn't her goal. Dodging his outstretched arms, she played a game of keep-away. And for a while she was successful until, laughing too hard, she lost her footing and fell to the sand. Sam tried to pin her beneath his body, but Megan squirmed and wiggled until they were both covered with sand. They lay exhausted, a tangle of arms and legs, their laughter subsiding only when he kissed her.

Lying next to each other on the warm sand, they watched the clouds race across the sky and were content to simply be with each other. It wasn't until Megan remembered a story her father had told her when she was a child that she broke their companionable silence. "Know how the Sleeping Bear Dune got its name?"

"No. Tell me."

"It's an Indian legend. Long ago, living way over there—" she turned on her side and pointed across the lake to a spot beyond their view "—in the state of Wisconsin, there was a mother bear and her two cubs. A terrible forest fire drove them into Lake Michigan and they began to swim for safety. They swam on and on, but the cubs grew tired and began to fall behind. The mother bear urged them to keep swimming, but she kept pulling ahead of them until finally she was so far ahead, she couldn't see them."

Megan then rolled to her stomach and pointed to the shoreline and the five-hundred-foot-high shifting sand dune that the park was named after. "At last the mother bear saw land and pulled herself out of the water and lay down there to wait for her cubs. Faithfully she waited, never leaving the spot. But the cubs didn't come because they'd grown too tired to keep swimming and had drowned.

"Then the great spirit Manitou took pity on the mother bear and her two cubs. He gave her eternal sleep and raised the twin cubs out of the water and made them islands— Manitou Island and South Manitou Island." Megan waved her hand toward the two islands off shore. "Then he covered the mother bear with sand, so all men would know of her goodness and patience."

Sam sat up, brushing the sand from his body. "It's a beautiful story, Megan. Too bad all mothers aren't so noble and devoted."

"You really resent your mother, don't you?" Megan also sat up. She could barely remember the time she'd resented her father. It seemed so long ago.

"I don't know if resent is the right word," he said pensively, standing and reaching down to give her a hand. "I know if you asked her, my mother would vehemently deny any personal motivation in the way she exploited me as a teenager. And she would rightfully point out that she put most of the money I earned into a trust fund, and that I owe the financial independence I now enjoy to her. Still, I find it very difficult to believe that anything she suggests is really for my good alone. I always suspect an ulterior motive. And that's a terrible way to think about your mother."

"I can't imagine that kind of a relationship. Even when my father and I were having those terrible arguments, I always knew, deep down, that what he was saying was for my own good."

Sam squeezed her hand and they started back toward their cottage. "One reason I decided to stay at The Quarter Note—besides a lust for your luscious body—was the camaraderie I sensed between you and your father. It was so good to see how much you cared for each other. I wanted to be around that for a while, share a bit of it." Leaning close, he kissed her. "It's nice."

It rained that afternoon and the next day and the next, but neither Sam nor Megan cared. They stayed in their cottage, where they talked and made love. He practiced on his guitar and she sketched him using pencil, pen and ink, charcoal and pastels.

"What's that you're playing?" she asked, the almost spiritual melody of the piece he was playing drawing her attention away from her drawing.

"The Andante from Beethoven's Sonata no. 4."

As his fingers knitted together the intricate sounds, the pure tone of the guitar adding an ethereal quality, the beauty of the piece overcame her. When he'd finished, Megan was at a loss for words. "That was so ... so ... beautiful."

Sam smiled from where he sat. "I think Beethoven poured his deepest and most poetic feelings into the movement. But I should be playing something more cheerful." He winked at her. "What we need is a love song." Immediately he changed to a livelier piece, singing aloud in Spanish.

"What does it mean?" Megan asked eagerly, after he'd played the last chord.

"It's an Andalusian love song. Our lover is asking his girl, as they stroll along, to tell him that she loves him. He says she may be afraid, but he, he's trembling with love."

"You said once that you were engaged to a Spanish woman. In fact, you were going to tell me about her when

Josh interrupted." Megan wondered if Sam had courted that woman with the same song and felt a touch of jealousy.

"And you'd like to know about her?" He teasingly raised his eyebrows as if the idea came as a great surprise.

"Yes," admitted Megan, wishing she didn't.

Sam began to play another piece. A strangely sad but beautiful melody. "Then I will tell you. Her name was Maria Luisa de Castillo, and I met her in Madrid. I was giving two performances there, after which I was scheduled to go on to Barcelona. Then I was going to take a month's holiday in Monte Carlo. Maria and I were introduced at a party given in my honor.

"I was twenty-four. It was my second trip to Spain, and I was quite impressed by my welcome. The Madrid press had given my arrival a great deal of coverage, and one magazine actually featured my life story. I was equally impressed to discover Maria had read everything about me. At twenty-two, she was a beautiful, sophisticated woman. Not your usual groupie. She told me it was an honor to be in my presence, but considering the number of men hanging around her, I felt I was the one being honored when she singled me out. Witty and intelligent, she spoke English well, and totally entranced me.

"She invited me to her home that night and for the next two days we were inseparable, but then I had to fly to Barcelona. I knew, even before I left Madrid, that I couldn't spend a month in Monte Carlo without Maria. When she said she couldn't possibly leave her ailing grandmother, I canceled my reservations, and after my performances in Barcelona I returned to Madrid. I was in love. Or I thought I was."

He studied Megan, wondering how she was taking all this. Her expressive gray eyes were locked on his face, her sensuous mouth a tight line. He found it difficult to go on, not wanting to hurt her. But he also felt she deserved to know about his past.

"For a month Maria and I went everywhere together. It was during that time I discovered how much Maria loved parties. At a party Maria always managed to become the center of attention; she thrived on it. And when someone from the press recognized me, she would slide her arm through mine and pose like a model. The next day she'd search the papers for our picture. If it wasn't printed, she'd fume. If it was, she'd cut it out and display it. Her bit of vanity amused me. I didn't really realize just how important it was for her to be in the limelight.

"We became engaged by chance. Someone asked when we were planning to be married—making a joke of how inseparable we were—and Maria said as soon as the banns had been read. I really hadn't thought about marriage at that point. We'd known each other such a short time and there was the difference of our religions to consider. But as soon as Maria made that announcement, it seemed to become a fait accompli.

"I bought her a beautiful engagement ring, and she showed it off to everyone. I even spoke to her priest and promised to take instructions as soon as I returned from my tour in Russia. That tour, unlike a holiday in Monte Carlo, was something I couldn't cancel. I was only going to be gone for six weeks. Maria said it would give her a chance to prepare for our wedding. So I left my bride-to-be, certain I was the luckiest man on earth."

He hated to admit how naive he'd been. "While I was in Russia, I received only two letters from Maria, but I wasn't concerned. Receiving mail while on tour in a foreign country isn't especially easy, and I was certain she was busy, getting ready for our wedding."

Sam hit a dissonant chord, and for a minute a lack of harmony hung over the room. Then he began again to play the beautiful haunting melody, and he went on. "I suppose, since I hadn't heard from her in weeks, I should have suspected something, but a man in love is blind. Desperate to see Maria again, I finished up in Moscow early and immediately flew back to Madrid. I arrived at Maria's unannounced, hoping to surprise her. I did. She was with another man. A bullfighter." Sam laughed bitterly. "Did you know in Madrid a bullfighter gets more publicity than a guitar player?"

"Sam..." Megan interjected, hurting for him. "You don't have to go on."

"Actually there's not much more to the story. I discovered that after my departure Maria had continued going to parties and that the bullfighter wasn't the only man she'd taken home. I informed her that I wasn't into sharing, told her to keep the ring and took the next flight out of Madrid."

Sam hit a final chord to indicate the conclusion of his story, and Megan sat and stared at him. At last she found the nerve to ask, "Do you still love her?"

"No." He shook his head. "And now I wonder if what I felt then was love, or if it was simply infatuation." Putting down his guitar, he moved over to where she sat cross-legged on the bed. Lovingly he kissed her lips and brushed his fingers through her hair. "She never made me feel as happy and contented as I feel around you."

"Oh, Sam—" her arms went around him and she squeezed him tight "—it's the same with me. Not once during that year I spent with Rod was I ever as happy as I've been these past few days with you."

Her drawing tablet was poking him in the ribs, and Sam pulled back, gave her one last quick kiss, then looked down at the drawing she'd been working on. "Enough of these soul-wrenching confessions. What have you done with me today?"

"I've been breaking you down into your simplest form, trying to see how few lines I need to clearly capture your features as well as show that you're playing the guitar. What do you think? Is it a success or a failure?" She handed him her sketchbook.

The tablet was nearly filled with drawings of him. Some were quick simple sketches to show the attitude and movement of his body when he was playing. There were a few realistic portraits, carefully drawn and shaded. She wasn't happy with any of them. And the rest were her more abstract renditions. The one she'd just finished fitted that category.

"Well?" Megan asked, wanting his opinion.

Sam studied the page closely. "I like it. May I have it?"

"Sure." She was pleased. Over the past few days he'd shown an acute understanding of what she was trying to accomplish. She'd found she could ask his opinion and he would give her a thoughtful critique, a careful analysis of a drawing's weaknesses and strong points. But never before had he asked for one of her drawings. Carefully she tore the page from her tablet and handed it to him.

"But it must have your signature." He handed the sketch back. "One day this will be worth a fortune."

"You have more faith in my future as an artist than I do." Megan laughed. "I sometimes wonder if I'll ever get out from behind that bar."

"Believe me, things are going to get better," Sam promised, carefully placing the picture in his guitar case.

"See what I mean. The sun's coming out. Let's go see if the water's calm enough for us to go sailing."

THE WEEK PASSED so quickly that Megan found it hard to believe their romantic interlude had come to an end. But as Sam packed the last of their luggage and souvenirs into the Porsche, she knew it would be only a few more hours before they returned to the realities of everyday living.

Leaving their private sanctuary was sad. Even though she'd missed her son and her father, Megan couldn't remember when she'd ever been happier. The time she'd spent with Sam had been filled with love and laughter. For seven days they'd shared the ultimate in physical and emotional intimacy, and if it was possible, she'd grown to love him more than before. The only thing marring her happiness was that November was now one week closer.

11

THE LOAN MONEY brought about rapid changes in The Quarter Note. By the last week in August the damaged areas had been repaired, the bathrooms and broom closet rebuilt, the entire bar rewired, an automatic sprinkling system installed, new carpeting laid in the lounge and the woodwork polished to a sheen. Not a trace of smoke or soot remained, the liquor stock had been replenished and a full array of cheese and sausages filled the cooler. The Quarter Note was scheduled to reopen September first.

"We're going to have to hire another bartender," Megan pointed out to her father. "At least until you get that cast off and your wrist is stronger. If we get any sort of a crowd, Pete will need some help during that last shift."

So they advertised for a temporary bartender.

Many people applied for the position, but only one impressed them. Carol Gardner, besides being a good-looking woman, radiated an enthusiasm and a zest for life that were contagious. She was a widow with two grown children and had just graduated from the bartending school in Grand Rapids. She told them honestly that she'd had no experience. She said she wanted the job because she thought she'd like working in a bar the size of The Quarter Note.

"Although I don't know much about tending bar, I liked the Gardner woman," Sam stated after the final interview.

"So did I," Megan agreed, leaning back against Sam as he rubbed her shoulders. "I think what she lacks in experience she'd make up for in her willingness to work. She's the kind of person we need at The Quarter Note."

"I liked her, too, but I don't like the idea of a woman driving home after two in the morning," muttered her father, pacing the floor and chewing on the eraser end of a pencil.

"Dad, she's the one who picked bartending as a career," Megan pointed out. "Certainly she realized she'd have to work late hours. Besides, she'd be a lot safer driving home from Shady Lake than she would be if she worked in Grand Rapids."

"She has my vote," added Pete.

So, despite Megan's father's reservations, Carol Gardner was hired. And Herb McGuire made it his personal duty to train her.

Megan had to smile whenever she saw her father hovering near the woman. "I swear he'd open the bottles for her if he could," she whispered to Sam. It was Carol's test run and they were pretending to be customers. Seated at one end of the bar the afternoon before the official reopening, they waited for Carol to bring their order.

"He likes her," Sam responded under his breath. "And I think she likes him."

Megan studied the woman more closely.

Carol Gardner was certainly attractive. Tall and leggy, her figure quite slender, she carried herself with poise and moved with a spring to her step. Her hair was dyed a soft honey blond, and only a few tiny crow's-feet near her expressive brown eyes hinted at her age.

Always smiling and laughing, Carol projected a natural sexuality that drew men to her. But a romance with her father? Megan shook her head. "Dad hasn't looked at a woman since Mom died. I'm sure he simply wants to make certain Carol does well."

"And I keep trying to get you into bed because I'm concerned about your health," Sam kidded. "Honey, your father's a man."

"He's nearly sixty," Megan argued, her gray eyes now taking in every smile, every gesture Carol made to Herb and, in turn, every gesture and smile he made to her. "What would she see in my father?"

Sam laughed. "Spoken like a true daughter."

"Something funny?" asked Herb, following Carol, who was carrying two drinks and a tray of assorted crackers and cheeses toward them.

"Depends on your point of view." Sam grinned at Megan, daring her to tell her father what they'd been discussing.

"Depends on how warped your sense of humor is," she returned. "How's it going, Carol? Know where everything is yet?"

"I think so. Your dad's really been helpful."

As she spoke, Carol placed cocktail napkins, with the quarter note motif Megan had designed, on the counter. She then set their drinks on top, placed the snack tray between them and cleaned Sam's ashtray. Every move was efficient and smooth.

What Megan noticed most was that Carol didn't even look at Herb when she mentioned him, and her expression was totally noncommittal. She decided Sam was wrong. Her father was simply a bar owner trying to make certain his new employee knew her routine. And Carol was simply an employee who was eager to do well. Romance was the furthest thing from either of their minds.

"I think we're ready," Herb said. He leaned on the counter, and Carol turned and walked back to the cash register. "You have everything set?" he asked Sam.

"All set," Sam answered.

"What's set?" asked Megan. For the past few days Sam and her father had been plotting something—a secret they wouldn't divulge.

"Your surprise birthday party," Sam teased, picking up a wedge of cheese and holding it in front of her lips as an offering.

"My birthday's not until next month." She nipped at the cheese, nearly catching his fingers.

"See what a surprise it will be?" He adopted a look of concern as he studied the tips of his nails. "Didn't anyone teach you not to bite the hand that feeds you?"

"You said your nails were getting too long."

"I meant I had to file them, not chop them off. Remind me never to ask you to cut my hair. I might lose my head."

"A tempting thought," Megan mumbled. "You're not going to tell me, are you?" She glared first at Sam, then at her father. "Neither of you."

"You'll find out tomorrow." Her father laughed, knowing that patience was not his daughter's strongest point.

The reopening had been publicized from Kalamazoo to Grand Rapids with the hope of attracting a crowd. By eight o'clock opening night, Megan knew they weren't going to be disappointed. The tables were jammed, the front bar was crowded and she was glad they'd asked Carol to come in early. The orders Nancy and the other cocktail waitresses were bringing definitely necessitated three bartenders.

Sam arrived at eight-thirty, guitar case in hand. Watching him come toward the bar, dressed in his familiar black shirt, slacks and boots, Megan remembered the first time he'd played at The Quarter Note. He'd told them he was a "pretty good guitar player." How little they'd known.

No longer did her stomach flip when she saw him. Instead, a warm, happy glow spread through her, and she welcomed him with a smile.

"Looks like a good crowd," he said, leaning on the counter near the cocktail waitresses' station and looking over his shoulder.

"It's fantastic—" Megan poured vermouth with one hand and gin with the other. "Better than—" she stopped pouring the vermouth, but went on with the gin "—I'd expected." Putting the gin bottle back in the speed well, she stirred the drink with a mixing spoon. "It's been hectic around here since seven." A quick dip in the clear sink rinsed her spoon, then she reached for the strainer and poured the martini into a cocktail glass. "They've been asking when you'd be in. You're still our biggest drawing card, you know."

"It's nice to be wanted." He grinned. "Give me a kiss for good luck."

Sam leaned toward her, and Megan obliged. Immediately two men seated at the bar applauded and demanded their turn. A touch of color reached her cheeks, but she covered her embarrassment with a laugh. "Sorry, only guitar players get kisses."

"My turn, then!" a man sitting farther down the bar yelled. When she gave him a questioning look, he lifted a battered guitar case.

"How's about banjo players?" another man asked, and he, too, held up an ancient, well-worn case.

Puzzled, Megan looked at Sam for an answer. She hadn't seen the men bring in the instruments. Since seven o'clock she'd been too busy to notice much about any of the customers.

"Fine thing, offering to kiss every guitar player in the place," Sam muttered. He pretended to be upset, but his blue eyes were twinkling with amusement.

"Sam, what is going on?"

"A possible solution to a problem."

"Whiskey sour, pina colada and a rusty nail." Nancy set her empty tray next to Sam's hand. "Hi, Sebastian, baby. Still messin' with the boss?"

"The lady pays my salary. How's it going?"

Nancy beamed and held up her left hand to let him inspect a small diamond solitaire. "Caught me a live one while you guys were cleaning up after that fire. Roy Van Camp. He may not be world famous, but he's a winner." Nancy grinned.

"Congratulations." Sam slid his arm around her slim shoulders and gave her an affectionate squeeze. "I wish you the best."

"The wedding's the end of this month. We'd like you to play for us, if you don't charge too much."

"For you, the charge would be nothing. But I can't," Sam apologized, "I've got to get back to New York."

He saw Megan tense, the color draining from her face, and he knew she'd overheard. He'd wanted to wait until they were alone to tell her. Now it was out. "We both knew I'd have to leave soon," Sam directed to Megan, not knowing how to soften the news.

"I . . . I didn't think it would be until November." Her words were barely audible above the noise in the lounge. "I . . ." Quickly she jabbed a pineapple slice into the pina colada, placed the glass on the counter next to the other two drinks and turned to ring up the bar tab.

"Megan?"

"It's all right." Her back to him, she took a deep breath and bit her lower lip to keep it from quivering. "I understand." The cash register rang up the total with a resounding clang. Turning back, Megan handed the bill to Nancy.

"Megan, we need to talk." He eyed her closely, not liking her frozen, lifeless expression.

Nancy discreetly picked up her order and melted into the crowd.

"Gimlet, pitcher of beer, three glasses and a cheese tray," another waitress ordered, immediately filling Nancy's spot.

Megan turned away from Sam and grabbed for the vodka and lime juice.

"Megan, take a break and talk to me," Sam insisted.

"I can't. I'm busy," she muttered, keeping her head down so he couldn't see the tears welling in her eyes.

"Ten o'clock. Out back. Don't go home without seeing me."

"With Josh staying at a friend's tonight, I'm working over. I'll be busy during your break."

"Pete and Carol can handle the bar. Ten minutes. That's all I'm asking."

"We're busiest during your break." Megan poured the beer without thinking about what she was doing. It foamed over the sides and onto her fingers. Quickly she grabbed for a towel and wiped off her hand and the glass pitcher. "I can't argue with you and work at the same time," she snapped and headed toward the cooler for the cheese.

Sam moved down the bar with her, wedging his way between a couple in their early twenties. "Honey, marry me. Come with me."

"Marry you?" She stared at him, not believing her ears. He'd asked her to marry him, to be his wife. They would go to New York together, take Josh and— Megan's idyllic thoughts came to an abrupt halt. She couldn't go. Not now. Not under the circumstances. Of all people Sam should understand how impossible that would be. Her daydreams had been replaced by anger. "I suppose you expect me to run out on my dad, like you are?"

"I'm not running out on your dad. And neither would you be."

"Sure. Tell me, who's going to take your place?" She waved her hand toward the tables of people. "You know as well as I do they come to hear you. Without you, The Quarter Note is just another bar—a bar that's too far from anywhere." Megan slapped cheese onto a tray and reached for a package of crackers. "Another month, maybe two, and things might have been okay. Why now, Sam? Why when we're just reopening?"

"Because I have to. I've been invited to play for the president."

"And I thought you were different."

She started to take the cheese tray to the cocktail waitresses' station, but Sam reached across the counter and caught her hand before she could move away. "I *am* different, and I'm not deserting you. People are going to come. Wait and see. You've got to think positive."

"Right," agreed the man whom Sam had separated from his date. Pointing to the cheese tray Megan was preparing, he asked, "Can I have one of those?"

At a loss for words, Megan stared at the man, then at Sam.

"We can't talk about this now...here." Sam nodded toward the back door and let go of her wrist. "I'll explain everything at ten."

He went back and picked up his guitar case, then slowly worked his way through the crowd, pausing at almost every table he passed to shake hands and chat with customers. Megan fixed a cheese tray for the man at the bar.

She was thankful for the orders being yelled at her; there was no time to think, no time to fully absorb the reality of what was happening. Like a zombie she mixed drinks, sliced summer sausage and cheese and rang up bar tabs. Only her father—supposedly standing by to help Carol, should she need any help—noticed that something was wrong.

"You feeling all right?" he asked, waiting for her to finish at the cash register so he could check the till for change.

"Fine," Megan said tightly.

"You look pale."

"It's warm in here."

He frowned, watched her hurry to start her next order, then shook his head and broke open a roll of quarters.

Sam began playing before nine o'clock. The entire barroom quieted with his first chords. "Good to see everyone back," he chatted, warming up with a rapid succession of arpeggios as he spoke. "Hope everyone appreciates the new carpeting and lights, and, of course, you must check out the fancy new commodes."

There was a titter.

"I think you're going to discover we've made a lot of changes here at The Quarter Note, but let's start out with an old favorite." Easily he moved into "Shenandoah." With the magical powers of his fingers, he enchanted them all, and as soon as that familiar piece was over, he switched to a hand-clapping, foot-stomping folk song from the sixties.

For at least half an hour Sam worked his audience, singing at times and getting them to sing along with him at other times. They loved it, and they loved him. A tear slid down Megan's cheek as she watched and listened.

Somehow she'd hoped the season would never end, and he would never have to leave. It had been a fairy tale summer, a time when dreams came true. Now it was time to wake up.

"Ladies and gentlemen, we're going to try something new tonight," Sam suddenly announced, and Megan wiped the tears away. This had to be what he and her father had been planning all week.

"For weeks I've been hearing that there's a lot of talent around Shady Lake. Many of you in the audience have told me about these people." He smiled. "Many of you in the audience *are* these talented people. So, starting tonight and from now on, every Thursday, Friday and Saturday night, The Quarter Note is going to give musicians—amateur or professional—a chance to play or sing. Each performer will get twenty minutes, and all you need to do is sign up with Herb at the bar. Show them where you are, Herb."

Herb waved his cast like a banner.

"Tonight, for a start, we called in a few musicians I'd been told about. Charlie? Charlie Gordon, why don't you come up and join me?"

The man from the bar, who had asked for a kiss, left his stool and, with his guitar in hand, made his way past the tables toward Sam.

Charlie Gordon had become a regular at The Quarter Note before the fire. He'd told Megan once that it was Sam's guitar playing he came to hear. Tall and lanky, his hands callused from hours of hard labor, his face wrinkled from too many years of working outdoors, Charlie Gordon hadn't resembled a musician to her.

He sat on a stool Megan hadn't even noticed was back by the piano, and for a few minutes, tuned his guitar to Sam's. Then Charlie and Sam began to play together, Charlie strumming the melody, Sam the accompaniment. The effect was rich and harmonious.

They played two pieces together, Charlie relaxing perceptibly the more he got into the songs. The third piece he played solo, until Sam broke in on the second chorus. They were jamming, having fun, laughing and improvising as they went along. And the customers loved it.

By ten o'clock Sam had also introduced Seth Armstrong, the banjo player. Charlie and Seth were old friends, and it was obvious they'd often played together. Their styles blended well, and neither musician seemed to notice when Sam stood up and leaned his guitar against the wall. He looked toward the bar, directly at her, then nodded toward the back door. He hadn't forgotten.

With a tug, Megan pulled off her bar apron. Fine. She'd talk. As if talking about it would help. He was going . . . going to play for the president of the United States. What could she say that would change that? She slipped away from the busy bar and headed for the exit.

The night was dark, only a sliver of a moon lighting the sky. And the wind that whipped through the trees and stirred up the lake held the distinct aroma of fall. Goose bumps rose on Megan's arms, but she wasn't sure if they were due to the weather or the cold dread that had invaded her heart. "When are you leaving?" she asked, as soon as the back door closed.

Sam had started to reach for a cigarette, but changed his mind and shoved the pack back into his shirt pocket. "I should be in New York in a week."

"So soon?" She'd hoped there would be more time.

"Yes." Sam closed the gap between them and wrapped his arms around her. "Besides this command performance, Cal's lined me up a recording date for the folk album and a concert after that."

"Isn't it awfully short notice?" She was angry... with the president... with Cal... with anyone and anything taking Sam away.

"Actually I had an idea last week that I was going to have to leave."

"Last week? You didn't say a word. Not one word."

"I didn't want to say anything until I was sure," he tried to explain. "Come with me when I go, Meg. Marry me."

She stared at him—at his blue, blue eyes and craggy features. His face was clearly illuminated by the yard light, his sensuous mouth so close and tempting. Oh, how she loved him. But that didn't change the way things were. "I can't," she said, ducking her head so his lips missed hers and grazed her temple, instead.

Surprise showed in his eyes. "Why?"

With Sam's arms around her it was difficult, but she tried to be logical. "Because as much as I want to be your wife—and believe me, I do—I can't leave until The Quarter Note's on its feet. And with you gone, this place is definitely going to have problems."

"Megan, I think this idea of using amateur talent is just what you need. It will be different. Unique. People will come to hear their friends play, to see who's here, to check out if they're any good."

"Maybe, but I still can't leave. Not while Dad needs me."

"Honey, believe it or not, your father can run this bar without you."

"No, you don't understand." She twisted in his arms so she faced the lake. The rough, windswept water mirrored her internal turbulance. "I took off once, thinking only about myself. I was still a child then. I'm a woman now. I have to think about others."

"And what about me?" Sam demanded. He turned her back, so she had to look at him. "I need you, too."

"Not like my father does. If Josh and I leave now, he'll be all alone."

"Unless you plan on living with him for the rest of your life, he's going to have to be alone someday. Think about Josh. He'll be starting school next week. If you marry me now, there's a private school for musically gifted children not far from where I live. Josh could attend as a day student and be able to learn any instrument he wanted. I've written to the director. I think they'll accept him."

"No," Megan cried, pushing herself away from Sam's embrace. "You know how I feel about that. How could you even think I would approve of such a school? I don't want Josh learning any instrument he wants. I don't like what I see already. All he thinks about is that guitar of his. Hour after hour, he plays it. It isn't normal."

"Megan, Josh isn't normal. He's gifted. I thought you'd faced that."

Backing up, she shook her head. "I said you could give him lessons, that's all. I don't want him growing up like—"

"Rod? Or me?" Sam's eyes narrowed as he stared at her. "I'm a musician. Remember? Would it be so terrible for Josh to turn out like me?"

"Yes!" Megan cried, and put her hands to her temples. "No. I don't know. I just know I don't want Josh going to a music school. I want him to grow up like every other normal boy, go to college, find a good job, get married—"

"All right, he won't go. He's your son. It's your decision." Sam said it calmly, but Megan heard the bitterness in his tone.

"You don't approve, do you?"

"No." He eyed her steadily. "Tell me, which is worse? A mother who forces her son to play, or one who keeps her son from playing?"

"That isn't fair. I'm not like your mother."

"Aren't you?" Sam's eyebrows rose sardonically.

"I'm doing it for—"

"Josh?" he finished for her. His cynical expression told her far more than his words.

"You're not even trying to understand."

"Oh, but I am. I've tried to understand your reasoning all summer. But I can't. You're condemning the son for the sins of the father . . . and the mother. When are you going to realize Josh is his own person?"

"Damn you!" Megan turned on her heel and started for the door, but Sam caught up with her and stopped her.

"Don't run out on me, Megan. I'm asking you to come with me, to marry me and be my wife. Despite our disagreement about Josh, I do love you."

She stared at the ground for a moment, gathering her thoughts, then turned and faced him. Far calmer than she felt, she gave her answer. "I love you, too, Sam, but sometimes love's not enough. It won't work." Shaking her head, the tears came to her eyes. "It just won't work."

12

FOR THREE DAYS Sam tried to convince Megan to marry him and move to New York, and for three days she gave him her reasons why she couldn't possibly go. It angered her that he couldn't, wouldn't, understand, that he was putting her in a position where she had to chose. "If you loved me, you'd understand," she cried.

"If you loved me, you'd want to be with me," he argued.

Finally the day came when Sam had to leave: They were still at an impasse, and Megan wasn't happy with the way things were turning out, but she saw no alternative. When Sam said goodbye, she promised to write, and he promised to answer her letters.

Tears streaming down her cheeks, Megan watched the Porsche disappear from sight, and once again she told herself she'd made the right decision, that she couldn't just run off and leave her father. But that night, as she lay alone in bed, none of her reasons for not going to New York helped ease the heartache.

Sam called her when he reached his house on Long Island and sounded so close that Megan couldn't really believe he wasn't in the guest cabin, waiting for her. Once again he asked her to marry him and come to New York, and once again she said she couldn't—not yet, not the way things were. She wasn't certain if it was hurt or anger that led him to hang up.

A month went by. She didn't write. She tried, but every letter she started ended up in the wastebasket. Words on paper seemed so inadequate, and the situation was no different. She didn't hear from him, either. The days were growing shorter, but seemed eternally long. Josh started school, her father had his cast taken off, Nancy married Roy Van Camp and the amateur talent nights at The Quarter Note were attracting customers. Although they were far from being financially solvent, The Quarter Note's future did look brighter than Megan had expected.

She kept herself busy and forced herself not to think about Sam. The hardest times were when Josh played his guitar, and when he mentioned Sam. "Why couldn't we go with him, Mom? He said he wanted us to."

"Because Grampa needs us right now."

"Grampa said you should have gone. I heard him. He said you should have married Sam."

"Grampa was being polite."

"Grampa was telling the truth. You should have married him and gone with him," her father said, stepping into the living room at that moment. In his hand he held a stack of mail, which included two manila envelopes.

"Dad, what's wrong?" Megan asked anxiously. He'd left for the bar only ten minutes before. It was time for The Quarter Note to be opened. Their regular Saturday customers would expect it.

"Nothing. I stopped by the post office and when I saw this—"

He handed Megan one of the manila envelopes. "I thought you might like it right away. It's from Sam." That was obvious from the return address. "I got a letter from him, too. Said his performance at the White House went well, and he's been busy, working on the folk music album. Josh, here's one for you." Herb handed his grandson the second manila envelope. "Looks like Sam went on a writing binge."

Both Megan and Josh tore their envelopes open. Josh pulled a glossy black-and-white photograph from his. "Wow! Nifty!" he exclaimed, holding up the picture for his grandfather and mother to see. "It's Sam with the president. Wait until I show this to the kids at school."

Megan barely noticed. Sitting down at the table, she stared at the photograph she'd pulled from her envelope, then quickly read the letter that had also been enclosed. Tears misted her eyes. Blinking hard, she again looked at the photograph, then at the check clipped to the back.

"Did he send you one, too, Mommy?" Josh asked, coming to her elbow and reaching for the picture she held. "Oh, neat, it's a drawing of him."

"He says it's going to be the cover of his folk album. Of course it will have writing across it when it comes out," Megan explained.

"It's one of your drawings, isn't it?" her father said, lightly resting his hand on her shoulder. He'd heard the catch in his daughter's voice and knew she was close to tears.

Megan nodded. "I did it while we were at Sleeping Bear Dune." She handed her father the check. "He even paid me for it." A tear slipped down her cheek. "He didn't have to. It's more than I ever would have charged him. And he said . . ." She couldn't go on.

"Yes?" her father prodded.

"He said he still loves me and misses me, that his days are empty without me, and—oh, Dad—" Megan put her head down on her arms and began to cry.

"Mommy, what's wrong?" Josh asked, his small hands touching her slumped shoulders.

"It's all right," his grandfather assured him. "Your mother needs a good cry and then she needs to make a few important decisions. Why don't you go outside and rake leaves while we talk?"

Josh looked at his sobbing mother, then at his grandfather and back to his mother. Finally, with one last pat on Megan's shoulders, he nodded and started for the back door.

As the door closed behind Josh, Herb pulled a chair up next to Megan's and sat down. Touching her arm with his large fingers, he sighed. "All right, young lady, enough feeling sorry for yourself. Dry your eyes and talk to me."

"I can't," she sniffed.

"Yes you can. And you will."

Megan turned her head slightly and looked at her father through dark, wet lashes. "Dad, you can't sit here talking to me. You need to get The Quarter Note opened."

"I'm sure the only two customers waiting for me are Alan and Jim, and they'll still be around when I get there. So no excuses. I want to know exactly why you're here crying your eyes out, and not in New York with a man who loves you and who you obviously also love."

"I can't just take off and leave you." Sitting back in her chair, she rubbed her eyes with a napkin and wiped her nose.

"Baloney! Give me one good reason why not."

"You need me."

His eyebrows rose, and he cocked his head. "Think you're that indispensable? That an old man like me can't make it without your help?"

"No, but—"

"But what?" he interrupted. "You've done more than enough. You gave up a business that was just getting on its feet, turned all your savings over to me to invest in this

bar, and for the past year plus you've put in more than
your share of hours being housekeeper, barkeeper and
accountant. You've paid your debt, not that you ever owed
me anything in the first place. Now it's time you start living your own life."

"But if I leave, you'll have to hire someone to take my
place. You can't afford another bartender right now."

"Maybe I can't and maybe I can. Yesterday I had three
calls from different people wanting to know about these
amateur nights we're having. And all three signed up for
next weekend. Besides that, I had two calls from customers, checking on performance times. This idea of
Sam's is working, honey. We're finally in the black." He
squeezed her arm. "As for bartenders—" Herb grinned.
"Remember Carol?"

"Carol Gardner?" She should. It had only been two
weeks since her father had been able to resume his bartending chores and they'd let Carol go. They simply
couldn't afford to keep her on.

He nodded. "She stopped by the other morning. Just to
say hi. She's looking for a job." His smile was almost boy-
ish. "I sort of miss having her around. She kind of bright-
ened up the place, didn't you think?"

"Dad?" Megan asked, her expression questioning.

"Well, she is an interesting woman, and very attractive."

Laughing, Megan took her father's hand in hers. "And
how does she feel about you?"

Herb McGuire lowered his eyes to look at the table, and
Megan would have sworn he blushed. "She says I'm quite
a fellow."

"Have you asked her out?" Megan couldn't believe she'd
been so blind not to see what was going on between her

father and Carol, especially after Sam had as much as told her that the chemistry was there.

"We're going to a movie Monday night." His gaze met hers. "That is, if you have no objections."

"Objections?" Megan laughed out loud. "I'm pleased as punch. I adore Carol. She's perfect for you."

"I rather think so myself." He beamed, then his mood again became serious. "But back to you. I don't want you worrying about The Quarter Note. If you leave, Carol can take your place. And, if that bar can't sustain one more bartender's salary, then we'll cut back on some extras we've been providing. But I really don't think we're going to have a problem. I think, from now on, things are going to get better and better. So no more using The Quarter Note as an excuse. Do you want to marry Sam or don't you?"

Her father had come right to the point, and Megan knew that that was the decision she had to make. "There's Josh to consider," she hedged.

"What about Josh?"

"The music. I still don't want him to be a musician."

Herb frowned. "Your mother didn't particularly want you to be an artist, but she was wise enough to know she had to let you try your own wings. I always thought you inherited her common sense. Sometimes, though, I wonder."

Megan stared at the tabletop and sighed. "I certainly didn't show any common sense when I ran off with Rod."

"Nope. That was strictly an emotional decision. And it got you into trouble."

"And my feelings about Josh becoming a musician like his father—"

"Are emotional," Herb broke in before Megan finished.

"Oh, Dad, I don't know." She shook her head. "I just don't know."

"But you do love him?"

Her eyes met his. "Yes. More than I ever thought possible."

"Then go to him. Now. Catch a plane tomorrow morning. You could be with him by afternoon."

Megan laughed. "If I don't die of fright when the plane takes off!"

THE AIRPORT LIMOUSINE dropped her in front of an imposing two-story white house. Massive Doric columns, classic architectural lines and perfectly manicured lawns and shrubbery gave the place a regal air. With her coat and purse in one hand, a suitcase and tote bag at her feet, Megan stood in front of the enormous oak door. From her purse, she pulled out the address she'd scribbled on a piece of paper before leaving Shady Lake, compared it to the six-inch black numbers above the door and, satisfied, reached forward to push the doorbell.

A stern-faced, gray-haired woman, wearing a pale blue dress and starched white apron, opened the door. "Yes?"

"Is Mr. Blake in?" Megan asked. "Sebastian Blake?"

"Who's calling?" the woman asked, her hazel eyes narrowing suspiciously.

"Megan. Megan McGuire."

For a moment the woman stared at her, saying nothing, then the harsh lines of her face softened and broke into a smile. "From Michigan!" she exclaimed, stepping forward and picking up Megan's suitcase and tote bag. "Come in. Come in. He's in the music room, practicing. Do you want me to tell him you're here or would you rather surprise him? He told me, if you should ever call, to put you right through." Her smile grew even wider. "I'd say this was a person-to-person call, wouldn't you?"

"Yes." Megan grinned. She couldn't help but respond to the housekeeper's obvious pleasure in seeing her there. "Person-to-person."

"My name's Esther. You can leave your things here." Esther pointed to a chair in the vestibule. "Go down this hallway, turn right and take the second door to the left. He'll be glad to see you."

Megan nodded, placed her coat and purse on the chair and started down the hallway. Soon she could hear the sounds of a guitar, the rapid arpeggios and clear tones drawing her directly to the room Esther had mentioned.

The door was open, and for a moment Megan stood on the threshold, staring across the room. Sam sat on a straight-backed chair, his left foot propped up on a wooden block, his shoulders and head slightly bent over his guitar as he concentrated on his playing. His fingers moved with such speed that Megan was amazed they didn't get entangled. The complexity of the piece he was playing was far beyond anything she'd ever heard him do, the crisp rhythm and firm accents beautiful to listen to. She didn't move until he finished, then she clapped, and with a start, Sam looked her way.

"Megan!" he cried, setting the guitar down and springing from the chair. "Where did you...how...?" Four long strides brought him across the room to her. "God, you look good." Taking her into his arms, he lifted her to her toes and kissed her long and thoroughly.

Megan laughed with joy when Sam finally released her lips and let her catch her breath. "That was worth the scare of a plane trip."

"You flew?" He gazed down at her, still not believing she was really there, in his arms. "You, the lady who's afraid of heights?"

"I've always said it would take something mighty important to get me on a plane." Her hand grazed his chin. "You're important."

He captured her fingers and kissed them, one by one. "I can't tell you how glad I am that you're here."

"I missed you," she murmured, lost in the blue of his eyes.

"Not half as much as I missed you." Lifting her into his arms, he spun her around once, then set her back on the floor. "Esther!" he yelled. "Esther, come here!"

Esther came quickly down the hall, her white apron flapping with each choppy step, her hazel eyes shining as she stopped in front of them. The affection the woman had for her employer was clear. "Yes, sir," she said, slightly breathless from hurrying.

"This is Megan." He draped his arm around Megan's shoulders.

"Yes, sir. I know." Esther nodded, grinning.

"She's going to—" Sam stopped in midsentence and directed his question to Megan. "Marry me?"

"Yes," Megan murmured and rested her head against his shoulder. Gazing up at Sam, she knew she'd made the right decision. She was loved by the man she loved, her son had eagerly accepted the idea of having Sam as his father and her father had sent her off with his blessings.

"Then welcome to your new home." Esther beamed. "It's going to be nice having another woman around here."

"I have a son," Megan warned.

"So Mr. Blake has told me," Esther continued, smiling. "A marvelous boy, he said. Very talented."

Megan felt Sam tense and knew he was concerned about her reaction to that statement. "We'll have to see how talented," Megan answered calmly. She still wasn't sure how she felt about Josh going to a special school, but she'd decided it wouldn't hurt to consider the possibility. Perhaps being in a milieu where his musical interests were encouraged would keep Josh in school longer. It certainly would be better than having him drop out, as his father had.

As Sam relaxed beside her, Megan placed her hand on his. "Why don't you show me around my new home?"

"I'd love to."

Esther left them and Sam started on the ground floor, taking Megan from the music room to a huge library, through an elegant dining room, huge living room and into Esther's realm—the kitchen, pantry and her quarters. When they entered an enormous recreation room and Megan saw the pool table and indoor swimming pool, she knew Josh was going to be ecstatic. And the yard out back was both spacious and beautifully landscaped. Never had she been in such an elegant home. Realizing it would soon be hers left her a little breathless. If Sam hadn't been beside her, the warmth of his hand in hers comforting and reassuring, she might have been frightened by the idea.

Slowly they ascended the curving staircase to the second floor. He showed her the guest rooms first. Five of them. "This one—" he motioned to a room decorated in pastels "—is my mother's. At least, it's the one she's stayed in the two times she's visited me. Josh can pick the room he wants to use from the other four, and one could be an art studio, if you wanted."

"I'm overwhelmed." Each room was so light and airy that any one would do well as a studio.

"And this will be our room." Sam closed the door behind them and stepped aside to give her time to look around. "I expect you'll want to redecorate it. Give it a bit of a woman's touch."

"I think I might," she said with a chuckle, noting the heavy pieces of furniture, the dark draperies and brown carpeting. It was a man's room. There was no doubt about that.

"This, though, stays." Sam walked over and fell back onto a kingsize waterbed with a glassed-in bookcase headboard. He motioned Megan to join him.

She approached the bed cautiously, watching the mattress undulate beneath his long form. "I've never slept on a waterbed before," Megan admitted.

"Ever done anything else on one?"

"No." She laughed as he lurched up and grabbed her, pulling her down on top of him. "Sam, what are you doing?"

"I'm attacking you. Do you realize how long it's been since I've been in bed with you?" He nibbled on her ear, gently pulling on the gold loop.

"With me, yes, but you've probably had women lined up in droves at your front door, falling at your feet, crawling into your—"

"There's been no one," Sam insisted, before Megan could finish. "How could there be? I love you, Megan McGuire."

"Oh, Sam." She snuggled close, resting her head on his shoulder and letting the gentle rocking of the mattress ease the tension from her body. She'd prayed it would be like this, that he wouldn't have changed, but she'd been worried. Now, in his arms, she knew he was the same compassionate man who had stolen her heart. "I love you so much."

"I can't tell you how much I've wanted to hear those words from you. When you didn't write—" He kissed her hard, his lips punishing her for the torture she'd put him through.

But his anger was short-lived. His mouth grew softer and more pliant by the second, until the long, lonely nights were forgotten, and the only memory that remained was the happiness they'd shared. Needing to touch her, he slipped her blue suit jacket from her shoulders and tossed it aside.

"Remember that dirty old man who chased you around Windmill Island?" he asked, his lips only a breath from hers.

"The one who embarrassed me in front of the tour guide and those people?" Megan's voice was husky, her breathing shallow and rapid.

"You would have thought he could have kept his hands off you—" Sam's hands roamed over the silky texture of her blouse, to her arms and back again "—but he couldn't."

"I didn't want him to." No more than she wanted Sam to stop now. Every stroke of his fingers ignited her, and Megan moved her hips sensuously against his. She could feel his arousal, and that fueled her desire to make love with him.

"I imagine you're very tired after your flight." His words were becoming ragged, his touch more enticing.

"Not too tired." Adjusting her weight on the ever-moving bed, she sat back so she could look at him. "Are you tired after all your practicing?"

"I could use a little time in bed." His eyebrows rose in question. "Want to join me?"

Megan grinned, then raked her fingers through his thick curls. "Seems I already have."

He pulled her back down so she was pressed against his length and kissed her with a longing tenderness.

He discarded her white blouse, then her bra, and for a while he caressed her breasts, bringing her nipples to erect points. Then he kissed them until Megan was writhing with pleasure. "Sam, please," she begged, "I want all of you."

He pulled his gray-tweed sweater over his head and flung it to the opposite side of his bed. His shirt, however, thwarted him, the buttons seemingly endless. "Damn," he swore, fumbling with yet another.

"Relax," Megan soothed and loosened his belt buckle. She felt him shudder and smiled. He was wound as tightly as she was. The last button of his shirt gave way under his fingertips at the same time as she lowered the zipper of his charcoal gray slacks.

When they were both undressed, he reversed their positions so he was on top and leaning over her. For a moment they said nothing, their eyes locked, the gentle waves of the bed rocking their bodies. Then he leaned closer. "I love you, Megan McGuire. More than you'll ever know."

"And I love you," she returned, her hands going around his neck.

Again and again they kissed, their lips blending in remembered harmony. His hands caressed her body with the touch of a master, and she responded like a perfectly tuned instrument. Slowly, surely, he brought her to a heightened pitch of intensity until she ached for fulfillment.

"Now," she cried and gripped his shoulders as he made her his. Clinging to him, she became a part of his rhythm, the movement of the bed heightening each sensation. "Yes, oh, yes," she groaned, her legs pressing against his, her fingers tightening their hold as her body found complete satisfaction.

"Oh, Megan," he gasped and gave in to his own pleasure.

Their bodies were damp with perspiration, their breathing uneven, but they laughed in joyous abandon and held each other close, the bed slowing its movement and surrounding them with its comfortable warmth. "It's good to have you here," Sam murmured, his hand brushing moist tendrils of hair away from her neck.

"It's good to be here."

"I would have come back for you, you know. I wasn't going to lose you. If I had to spend the rest of my life at Shady Lake, I would have."

"Perhaps we could spend part of our summers there," she said, rolling to her side and starting the bed moving again. The motion was becoming pleasantly familiar.

"Maybe even part of our winters. I've been wanting to learn how to cross-country ski. How's the amateur night idea going?"

"Good. And I hate to admit it, but you were right about Carol and Dad. I believe my father's in love."

"Carol's a nice lady." Contented, he caressed Megan's back and shoulders. His eyes were nearly closed when she raised herself on one elbow, setting the bed in motion again.

"Sam, why didn't you tell me you loaned Dad the money to rebuild The Quarter Note?"

Opening his eyes, he tensed. "Because I was afraid you would object if you knew."

"Of course I would have objected. You did enough for us last summer without giving us money."

"I didn't give it to your dad—I loaned it to him."

"At the standard rate of interest? Or like you loaned me money for Josh's guitar?" The check she'd given Sam before he left Shady Lake still hadn't been cashed. "Dad sent a check with me. And this one I insist you cash. It's the money the insurance company paid us. But I have a feeling we owe you a lot more than that. Am I right?"

"Ask your dad," Sam hedged.

She had, just the night before, when her father first admitted borrowing the money from Sam. "You two," she grumbled, then laughed, in spite of herself. "Dad said to ask you."

"Your dad and I have everything worked out," Sam assured her, "so don't worry. I'm not going to lose any money, and my motive wasn't all that saintly." He pulled her close and kissed her. "I knew if I loaned your dad that money you wouldn't be tied up with cleaning that sooty bar, and I could get you all to myself for a little while."

With a smile, Megan remembered their week together. "Lecherous old man."

"Careful." He grinned. "Don't forget, you just celebrated a birthday. I'm not that much older than you now, so if I'm a lecherous old man, what's that make you?"

"A lecherous old lady?" Snuggling close, she rubbed her breasts against his chest.

"What a pair we'll make." A tightening of his groin made him forget about sleep, and the bed began to undulate as he moved across her body.

The sun was beginning to set when Sam finally helped Megan out of bed. "Have anything fancy you could wear tonight?"

"Like what?" She hadn't really known what to pack.

"A nice cocktail dress. Maybe something with a long skirt."

"I brought a white jersey. It's fairly dressy and has a long skirt." It had been a last-minute decision.

"Good." Sam smiled and led her toward his bathroom. "Because tonight I'm playing at Carnegie Hall."

"Sam," Megan gasped, holding back and staring at him. "Why didn't you say something. I mean . . . shouldn't you have been practicing . . . doing something?"

"I was doing something," he assured her, "and thoroughly enjoying myself doing it. In fact, my biggest problem before a concert, usually, is that I get too tense. Believe me, my love, tonight I'm relaxed."

They showered while Esther pressed Megan's jersey. Esther also brought sandwiches and coffee to the bedroom, which they ate and drank while they dressed. Megan helped Sam with his cuff links and he zipped up her dress. Time was short. "Really, you should have said something," Megan scolded, as Sam took her hand and hurried her down the stairs.

"Why ruin a good thing. Thank you, Esther," he said to his housekeeper as the older woman handed him his overcoat, then his guitar case.

Esther, in turn, helped Megan with her coat. "The limousine is waiting," she informed Sam and opened the front door.

Sam said little during the ride to the concert hall. Megan knew his mind was now on the performance he was about to give. She felt guilty and worried that her unexpected visit had been ill timed, that his performance would be less than perfect because of his afternoon's activities. Yet, selfishly, she didn't regret one moment they'd shared.

He arranged for her to have a front row seat and, with a kiss, left her. Nervously Megan looked around as the hall began to fill. She could tell it was an elite audience. The women were dressed in beautiful designer gowns, the men in dark suits and tuxedos. From the program in her hand Megan read that this was a special performance—a charity benefit. Ticket prices, she imagined, had been astronomical.

Finally the room was filled, the lights were dimmed and the audience quieted. A dark-haired woman in a sequined gown and stunning hairdo stepped to the center of the stage, tested the microphone, then welcomed all and announced that from the evening's proceeds twenty thousand dollars would be donated to the Special Olympics.

Applause followed her statement, then died as she raised her hands. "And now," the woman went on in her cultured voice, "the moment we've all been waiting for. An evening with Sebastian Blake."

Sam stepped on stage, his guitar in hand, bowed, and a wave of applause carried him to the woman. He lightly kissed her cheek, nodded at something she said and turned to watch her walk off stage. The applause increased in volume until he moved to the lone chair, center stage, and sat down. Sam then adjusted the block for his left foot, positioned his guitar and waited.

The applause ended, and there was a sporadic cough here and there. The entire hall vibrated with a sense of anticipation. "I will first play 'Gavotte' by Bach, from his Sonata no. 6 for violin in E Major partita, as transcribed by Andrés Segovia," Sam announced, and began to play.

Megan loved the sound of his voice—assured, clear and deep—his slight accent so familiar. Dressed in his black tuxedo, a black bow tie above the pleats of his starched white shirt, he exuded an air of self-confidence. And the clear, crisp notes that emanated from his guitar strings showed no hesitancy, no lack of vibrancy or strength.

With a smile, she watched him. She was going to be this man's wife: the wife of Sebastian Augustino Blake, guitarist. Strange how a few months could change one's point of view. Somehow musicians didn't seem such a bad lot, after all. At least, not some of them. And perhaps it wouldn't be all that bad if her son did decide to be a musician. Even though Josh had inherited his talent from his father, look who was going to be influencing him. Megan couldn't think of anyone she would rather have her son emulate.

If Sam thought a music school would be good for Josh, then they would enroll him. Sam was right. It was time she stopped fighting the inevitable. Under her breath, Megan chuckled. She'd make a bet, after ten years of listening to Josh bang and thump, that one of the instruments he took up would be the drums. What a combination—drums and guitar. Good thing Sam owned a big house. And, considering that neither of them had thought to take any precautions that afternoon, there might soon be more than one child prodigy running around. Not that that bothered Megan. A baby—Sam's baby—would be a wonderful addition to their life.

Sam finished the selection, and the applause was thunderous. He nodded in appreciation, then paused and looked her way. "I love you," he mouthed, and the joy and happiness she'd been feeling all evening swelled in her heart. Silently she said the words in return.

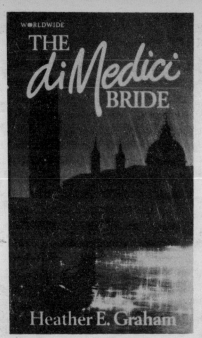

WORLDWIDE

THE *di Medici* BRIDE

Heather E. Graham

A marriage for romance or revenge?

Twenty-one years ago Mario di Medici was murdered at sea. Many suspected it was James Tarleton's hand that had pushed him over the rail.

When his daughter, Chris Tarleton, came to Venice, the riddle of the past returned with her.

Before she knew how, she found herself married to Marcus di Medici, the dead man's son.

Was his marriage proposal intended to protect her from the shadowy figure that followed her every move?

Or was his motive revenge?

WORLDWIDE

Another title from the Worldwide range.

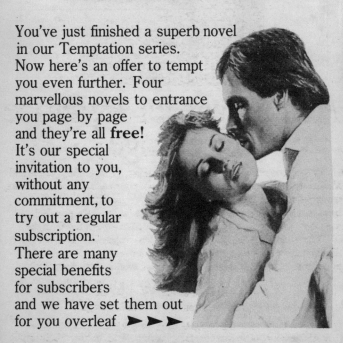